My Life
the Musical

By

Maryrose
Wood

Delacorte Press

Published by Delacorte Press
an imprint of Random House Children's Books
a division of Random House, Inc.
New York

Delacorte Press and colophon are registered trademarks of Random House, Inc.

Visit us on the Web! www.randomhouse.com/teens

Educators and librarians, for a variety of teaching tools, visit us at
www.randomhouse.com/teachers

Library of Congress Cataloging-in-Publication Data
Wood, Maryrose.
 My life, the musical / Maryrose Wood. — 1st ed.
    p. cm.
 Summary: Sixteen-year-old Emily Pearl's obsession with Broadway shows, and one musical in
particular, lands her in trouble in school and at home, but it might also allow her and her best
friend, Philip, to find a dramatic solution to their problems.
  ISBN 978-0-385-73278-9 (trade)
  ISBN 978-0-385-90297-7 (glb)
  [1. Musicals—Fiction. 2. Theater—Fiction. 3. High Schools—Fiction. 4. Schools—Fiction.
5. Broadway (New York, N.Y.)—Fiction.] I. Title.

PZ7.W8524My 2008
 [Fic]—dc22
                                                            2007015034

The text of this book is set in 11.5-point Goudy.

Printed in the United States of America

10 9 8 7 6 5 4 3 2 1

First Edition

★ ACKNOWLEDGMENTS ★

Thanks go, first, to editor Jodi Keller, for her patient and probing guidance, and to Beverly Horowitz, for her passion and encouragement to get it right. A special spotlight shines on Marissa Walsh, at whose suggestion this book was begun. I clap my hands madly for Colleen Fellingham, for her careful copyediting, Jason Zamajtuk, for the eye-catching cover design, and everyone at Delacorte.

This year and every other year, the Tony for Best Agent goes to Elizabeth Kaplan. Stellar reviews are garnered by my loyal posse of early readers, for their support and invaluable feedback: Andrew Gerle, E. Lockhart, Kate Herzlin, and Mana Allen. The eleven o'clock number of gratitude goes to Dave Shine, for decades of friendship and countless enjoyable postshow discussions over dumplings!

If I were to stand center stage and name all the mentors who have taught and inspired me personally and professionally over the years, the curtain would never come down. Instead, I offer a most inadequate, all-encompassing thanks to my many talented colleagues in the world of the theatre: actors, directors, musicians, designers, teachers, collaborators, my brave fellow writers (especially my pals in the BMI Musical Theater Workshop), and the few, the happy few, who persist in producing and nurturing new writing for the stage—you know who you are, and I hand each of you a large and expensive bouquet.

For all the Broadway composers, lyricists, and book writers mentioned on these pages, whose work will eternally delight, I leap to my feet in a standing ovation. Of these, I would like to warmly thank Stephen Sondheim and Sheldon Harnick, and also Richard Maltby, Jr., all of whom have been generously supportive of my own writing for the theatre.

A solo curtain call goes to Sal Allocco, who taught me so much: how to listen to Puccini, why Agnes is flaming, how to sing very fast while making a meat pie, and what to do when I'm "Losing My Mind." (The answer: stand in the light and belt!)

The final, company bow is for all my brothers and sisters from the original cast of *Merrily We Roll Along*, the most unforgettable entrée to Broadway a kid from Long Island could hope to have. Here's to us!

To members of the drama club,
everywhere

Overture

"ANOTHER OP'NIN', ANOTHER SHOW"

Kiss Me, Kate
1948. Music and lyrics by Cole Porter,
book by Samuel and Bella Spewack

BwayPhil: And it's . . . five minutes! The call is five minutes!

AURORAROX: 7:55! I didn't even start homework yet! Trigonometry evil, hate trig soooooo much . . . after the overture can you IM me some answers, pweeeeze???

BwayPhil: Emily, if you don't learn how to do it yourself, you will crash and burn on the final.

AURORAROX: *pleading expression on face*

"When a friend calls,
a friend must answer,
When the music starts,
become the dancer"

1

AURORAROX: so send me the answers I BEG of you

BwayPhil: Sheesh, if you're going to **sing** about it . . . ok but just this once.

AURORAROX: once will "never be enough," ha!

SAVEMEFROMAURORA: Shouldn't that be "danswer"?

BwayPhil: Can it be? The Aurorafans of Rockville Centre chat room gains a new member!

AURORAROX: "danswer"?

SAVEMEFROMAURORA: To rhyme with answer. Danswer. Get it?

AURORAROX: got it

AURORAROX: it's just sort of

AURORAROX: you know

AURORAROX: STUPID

AURORAROX: no offense

BwayPhil: Don't be rude, Emily! She means "welcome, new person."

SAVEMEFROMAURORA: No stupider than Aurora.

BwayPhil: Ouch, taking back the welcome . . .

AURORAROX: I don't like the tone

AURORAROX: of your tone

AURORAROX: new person

SAVEMEFROMAURORA: You're right. Stupid is the wrong word. How about banal, sophomoric, clichéd—

SAVEMEFROMAURORA: Loud. I forgot loud.

BwayPhil: Are you lost? This is the Aurorafans of Rockville Centre chat room, planetbroadway.com?

AURORAROX: FANS

AURORAROX: get it?

SAVEMEFROMAURORA: "Aurora" is no "Guys and Dolls," is all I'm saying.

BwayPhil: "Sit down, SAVEME, you're rocking the boat," is all I'm saying.

SAVEMEFROMAURORA: Cute! Score one for Phil.

AURORAROX: maybe you should see Aurora

AURORAROX: a few more times

AURORAROX: with an ***open heart***

SAVEMEFROMAURORA: I've seen Aurora plenty, thanks.

AURORAROX: so have we,

AURORAROX: but plenty will "never be enough"

AURORAROX: (that's a song from the show, just so ya know)

SAVEMEFROMAURORA: And just how many times have "ya" seen it, Miz Rox?

AURORAROX: ☺ would you care

AURORAROX: to take this one, BwayPhil?

BwayPhil: We're definitely approaching three figures.

BwayPhil: For an exact count I'll have to open my spreadsheets, it'll just take a minute . . .

SAVEMEFROMAURORA: turning blue—grabbing heart medication—

SAVEMEFROMAURORA: Kids—you are kids, right?—Please, get a life, okay?

AURORAROX: now that we've chatted

AURORAROX: & gotten to know each other

AURORAROX: i feel i can say this to you, SAVEME

AURORAROX: GO AWAY

SAVEMEFROMAURORA: I'm serious. Don't waste your time and money. I know what I'm talking about.

BwayPhil: Adios, SAVEME. Crappy screenname, BTW.

AURORAROX: LOL! {{{{philip}}}}

AURORAROX: whew, he's gone

BwayPhil: Now attention, ***true*** Aurorafans, it is now 8:02 . . . a mere twenty-five miles away, at the Rialto Theatre on West 44th Street in New York City . . .

BwayPhil: . . . the overture for performance #1013 of Aurora is about to begin! Places, the call is places please! Get your CDs ready . . .

AURORAROX: got mine.

BwayPhil: Got mine! On my count, press PLAY. 5 – 4 – 3 – 2 – 1

1

"ROCK ISLAND"

The Music Man
1957. Music, lyrics, and book by Meredith Willson

Sometimes—pretty often, in fact—sixteen-year-old Emily Pearl wished that her life were a musical.

A fabulous Broadway musical, she'd think. *With me as the star.* And every Saturday morning when she and Philip took the Long Island Rail Road from Rockville Centre into Manhattan to see the matinee performance of *Aurora*, the thirty-eight-minute train ride would magically transform into a toe-tapping, finger-snapping, Broadway-style production number.

The *chug-chug-chug* of the train would set the tempo. The conductors would tap-dance down the aisles, punching holes in the passengers' tickets to a syncopated beat. The babies would cry in key, the ringing cell phones would coalesce into a catchy melody, and soon the passengers would be swinging from the overhead luggage racks and belting out a happy traveling tune.

"Penn Station!"

That's how the number would end, with everybody singing very loudly, in lots of harmony parts.

"Penn Station!
Next and last stahhhhhhhhhhp!"

Thunderous applause.

Emily blinked and looked around. The train was as it always was, noisy and filled with sour-faced people reading the newspaper. The last note of the musical number was still ringing in her mind. It would take only the tiniest provocation, she felt—someone humming the right note, or gesturing in a particularly theatrical way—to cast the spell that would make it truly begin. She nudged Philip with her foot.

"Philip?"

"Hmmm?" Philip was busy updating the *Aurora* spreadsheets. These meticulously kept records chronicled every performance of *Aurora* the two of them had seen, all the way back to the first preview nearly three years before. Data categories included the weather, the exact locations of their seats, whether there were any understudies on, and anything unusual that might have happened during the performance (sometimes an actor flubbed a lyric or something went wrong with the set—mishaps like these were always terribly exciting in live theatre).

"Show question."

"Shoot."

"Has there ever been a *musical number*," Emily asked, staring dreamily out the train window at the little suburban houses flitting by, "a *production* number, that took place on a moving train?"

"Easy," he said. "*The Music Man,* opened on Broadway 1957. Book, music, and lyrics by Meredith Willson—two L's. The opening number is called 'Rock Island.' It takes place on a train and it's not even sung; it's spoken in rhythm." Philip smiled. "Great show. Rarely has a triple-threat author created a work that succeeds so well on all three levels: book, music, and lyrics."

It only took Emily a second to remember what Philip meant by "triple-threat." Most musicals had a composer, who wrote the music; a lyricist, who wrote the words to the songs; and a book writer, who came up with the story and wrote the script. Some shows had music and lyrics by one person and book by another, and some had music by one person and book and lyrics by another. But rarely did one person do all three jobs. There was no rule against it as far as she knew; Emily supposed it was just too hard to be good at everything.

"*Aurora* succeeds on all three levels," she said, somewhat defensively. She'd been feeling protective of the show since their weird encounter in the chat room with that SAVEME-FROMAURORA jerk. Banal? *Aurora?* Please.

"Yes, but nobody knows if *Aurora* was written by one, two or three people." Philip finished tallying some numbers in his head, jotted the answer on his spreadsheet, and looked up. "Who knows, it might even be more than three. *A Chorus Line* was based on interviews with the entire original workshop cast. *The 25th Annual Putnam County Spelling Bee* was partly derived from group improvisations." He was prepared to give more examples, but Emily didn't need to hear them.

Instead, she started singing softly to herself.

> *"Never be enough,*
> *My love for you could never be enough,*
> *Ten thousand years could never be enough*
> *To say what's in my heart. . . ."*

Emily sang in time with the rhythm of the train as she took a notebook and pen out of her messenger bag. The bag, a Hanukkah gift from her parents, had the familiar *Aurora* logo printed on it: a silhouette of the show's star, the divine Marlena Ortiz, her mittened hands reaching up to the sky and a long multicolored scarf twirling ribbonlike in the air around her. Emily started to write.

"Whatcha doing?" murmured Philip, perusing his copy of *Variety*, the weekly show-business newspaper. Last week *Aurora*'s ticket sales had dipped slightly, but the weather had been horrible. Funny how things like that made a difference.

"I need a 'persuasive essay' for English comp on Monday." Emily tapped her pencil eraser against her lower lip. "And I just figured out what my subject is."

Philip frowned. "Didn't Henderson tell you not to write about the show anymore?"

"It's not about the show." She leaned forward, bright-eyed with inspiration. "I'm going to write about Aurora. Aurora *herself*. The person who *wrote* the show."

"I don't see the difference, it's still *Aurora*." Philip didn't look up from his *Variety*. "Besides, nobody knows who wrote the show. Except whoever it was, of course."

"Hmmph," said Emily, undeterred. "But somebody *did* write it, that's the point! 'Aurora, By Herself.' That's what it says in the *Playbill*, and on the posters, and on the marquee. There *is* an Aurora, somewhere."

"True, but Henderson might not see it the same way."

"This is a persuasive essay," said Emily, a mad gleam in her eye, "and I'm going to persuade the reader that Aurora, the *real* Aurora, is actually two people: a collaborative team of composer-lyricist and book writer." She thought for a moment. "Or maybe it's a composer and lyricist–book writer, I'm not totally sure. But one of them is a man, no older than thirty, with a rural background but highly educated. The other is a woman, not from the United States, often depressed, perhaps a former actress . . ."

The train had gone into a tunnel now, and the lights flickered off and on the way they always did at such moments. Emily didn't notice. She continued spinning her theory, basing it on "hints" and "clues" she found in the dialogue and lyrics, costumes and staging of the show. Some of these "hints" she elevated to "compelling evidence," and only one time did she use the word "proof." She thought that showed a lot of restraint, which Mr. Henderson was bound to appreciate.

Philip gave up trying to dissuade her and spent the rest of the trip neatly stowing his spreadsheets, highlighters, and freshly sharpened pencils in his backpack. There was no point in trying to reason with Emily about *Aurora*. Her all-consuming love of Broadway musicals, like his, was as fixed and inevitable as the carefully scripted, rehearsed, choreographed, spotlit, and underscored shows themselves. Real life was a dull, chaotic mess by comparison.

"Penn Station, next and last stop," crackled the conductor's voice over the speakers. "All passengers must leave the train. Penn Station, last stop."

Emily and Philip had arrived. New York City, home of Times Square, Broadway, the Rialto Theatre, and *Aurora*.

2

"SUR LA PLAGE"

The Boy Friend
1954. Music, lyrics, and book by Sandy Wilson

Playing "stump Philip" was the preferred way to kill time on the *Aurora* rush ticket line. A steady steam of questions arrived, some verbally, some written on scraps of paper and passed down the line from person to person. Some days Philip declared a theme: Rodgers and Hammerstein shows, for example, or shows of the 1930s, but today he was only fielding questions about *Aurora*.

"How many performances have there been to date?" (A little under three years' worth: 24 previews, 989 performances, total 1,013.)

"How many fake flower petals are released over the audience each night during the curtain call?" (Roughly a ton per performance, eight tons a week.)

"How many musicians are in the pit?" (Twelve, plus four "pit singers," who sang along with the chorus when the on-stage performers got breathless from trying to sing and dance at the same time.)

"How much did the show initially cost to produce?" (Six and one half million dollars.)

There were many facts about *Aurora*, and Philip knew them all, but his personal favorite was the length of each performance. The first act of *Aurora* ran sixty-six, sixty-seven, or sixty-eight minutes, depending on how much applause there was. The second act ran fifty-nine or sixty minutes. Intermission was always sixteen minutes. The figures never varied, which Philip found extraordinary, since when his mother went to work on a Monday and said "See you later," sometimes it meant later for dinner and other times she didn't come home for two days because of a business trip to Wilmington that she'd forgotten to mark on the calendar.

"Hey," said Emily, tugging at his sleeve. "Check it out, Ian's back from Florida."

Together they looked down the rush line, which formed every Saturday morning in front of the theatre and snaked down Forty-fourth Street until it turned the corner on Eighth Avenue. If you arrived before ten a.m. with cash and had the fortitude and strong bladder to wait in line until one p.m., when the rush tickets were distributed, you might get one of the thirty discounted tickets that were put aside for Saturday matinees. Thirty tickets, day of performance only, first come, first serve. They were bad seats, too, upstairs and all the way to the side, but for twenty-five dollars who could complain?

In theory, the goal of the rush line was to make sure nonwealthy people could afford to go to the theatre. In practice, the thirty tickets almost always went to some subset of the hard-core Aurorafans, all of whom had seen the show dozens of times. It was a strange club, with its own cliques and factions, and Emily and Philip considered themselves among its more reasonable members.

From a half block away, Ian spotted them and waved. He broke into a graceful, waltzing skip and proceeded to pas-de-bourrée down Forty-fourth Street until he arrived at their spot on the line.

"Emily! Philippe! *Mes amis!*" He gave Emily a pair of Euro-style kisses, one on each cheek, and a somewhat more manly high five was exchanged with Philip.

"How was *The Boy Friend?*" asked Philip.

"Duh-READful show!" Ian said happily. "And the Florida audiences were, shall we say, elderly! But it was great fun spending winter break *sur la plage*"—he cast his eyes downward in a winning imitation of humility—"and I am now the owner of . . . it's such a small matter, I can hardly bring myself to say it . . ."

"A fake tan?" laughed Emily. "A shuffleboard trophy?"

"No, you suburban wench! An Equity card!" Ian threw his fists in the air and started singing the theme song from *Rocky*, except with these words: "I am a man with an Equity card! I am a man with an Equity card! Equi, Equi, Equi-ty card!"

If my life were a musical, thought Philip, with a deep rumble of feeling that was not unlike envy, *I'd start singing right along with him*. But Ian was an actor and could behave like a fool in public; it was expected. Philip had no desire to perform. He was a numbers man, and left the carrying-on to others.

"Ian! That is so awesome!" Emily jumped up and down in

celebration. "Just wait! You'll be on Broadway before you know it."

"I'm nervous, actually." Ian shoved his hands into his pockets against the chill. "Going pro really means 'Hello, un-employment.' I've worked at every non-Equity summer stock company on the East Coast, but those days are gone. Now I have to hold out for union work. Compete against the stahhhhs."

Philip punched him playfully in the arm. "C'mon, you're not even out of high school yet, and you made the union. You're way ahead of the game."

"Says you!" Ian said, pouting. "I swear, I am the only member of LaGuardia's senior class who hasn't done a *Law & Order* episode yet. I know I nailed the audition. I even scared myself. *Bam! Bam!*" Ian lunged murderously at Philip, then took an imaginary shot to the midsection and crumpled to the sidewalk in a limp heap. Emily and Philip applauded politely.

"Hey, *Olivier*, the line forms in the *rear*." The tall, absurdly dressed woman had her hands on her hips and a very threatening look on her face, but her fuzzy mittens and the pink glitter heart painted on her cheek pretty much spoiled the effect.

Ian sprang back to life and brushed off his jeans. "Chill out, Daphne! I'm not cutting the line, I'm just providing a little entertainment for my compadres, here. *Love* the outfits, by the way."

Daphne and her friends were the kind of Aurorafans who dressed up in faux *Aurora* costumes to see the show. On the girls one saw a lot of knit caps and goofy scarves mixed with fishnet tights and spike heels. On the guys, it was all about distressed leather jackets, round-rimmed John Lennon glasses, and two days' growth of beard, with a pout of soulful,

I'm-about-to-sing-a-ballad yearning inscribed on each Auro-rafied face.

"Can you stand it?" Ian muttered to Emily and Philip. "So *Rocky Horror*. Blech."

Emily couldn't agree more, though it was true that she'd once bought herself a striped scarf at a thrift shop. It had been an impulse, really, and she only tried the scarf on occasionally, at home, when she was alone. She was almost positive she'd never mentioned this to Philip.

"So how come you're not seeing the show today?" Philip asked Ian, as Daphne and her gang returned to their heated debate about whether there ever would be—or ever should be—a film version of *Aurora*. "After being away and all. Didn't you miss it?"

"*Bien sûr!* But I have a vocal coaching at two and dance class at four." Ian shoved his hips sideways in a distinctly Fosse-esque pose, which he dropped just as abruptly. "Next Saturday for sure—we'll get tickets and do lunch at the Edison. I'll try to get Stephanie to come, too."

"Awesome," said Philip quickly.

Stephanie Dawson was a petite, redheaded dancer with huge green eyes and a bright soprano voice. She'd attended LaGuardia High School of Music & Art and Performing Arts in Manhattan, better known as the *Fame* school, where aspiring performers trained their fannies off in the hopes of becoming stars. After graduating the previous June, Stephanie had promptly been cast as a replacement in the chorus of *Aurora*. She and Ian were good friends; in fact, last year, when she was a senior and he was a junior, they'd costarred in a school production of *She Loves Me*.

Stephanie was only nineteen but she was a pro, working

on Broadway and in *Aurora* no less, and this made her the nearest thing to a celebrity Emily and Philip had ever met. On three occasions Ian had brought Stephanie to have a quick lunch with them at the Café Edison before the matinee, and they'd been utterly dazzled. Emily suspected that Philip might have a crush. He seemed to stammer and turn pink and act even more geeky than usual in Stephanie's presence.

Emily both liked and disliked seeing Philip in this state.

> *Never understand,*
> *The rest of them will never understand,*
> *A love so far beyond*
> *The love that we had planned . . .*

Despite the vast stacks they already owned, Philip and Emily always took fresh *Playbills* when they walked into the Rialto Theatre. Each month when the new issue appeared, and the feature articles and star profiles and fawning little restaurant reviews changed, it was always cause for delight.

They read every issue cover to cover, even though Ian had told them it was mostly paid publicity. So what if it was? The magazine's pages were filled with juicy tidbits, and this much Emily and Philip understood: if Broadway had its own currency, it would be little razor-edged coins made of fresh gossip. Failing to keep up with the latest meant you were flat broke.

Philip flipped the pages and was disappointed: there were the same breathless articles from last week about Chita Rivera and Donny Osmond and the Don't Tell Mama piano bar, where anybody—seriously, anybody—could walk up to the piano, grab the mike, and belt out a show tune. Even so, Philip tucked the *Aurora Playbill* carefully in his bag, to add to his collection.

Few people, if any, had spent as much time quantifying, measuring, and dissecting *Aurora* as Philip had. What he'd discovered was that the facts and figures, consumed wattage and gross poundage of *Aurora* did absolutely nothing to prepare you for the experience of seeing the show itself.

Every Saturday afternoon it swept over him once more. The lights went down, the music played, and all at once Philip believed, to the core of his being, that these were real people on the stage. They sang and danced, laughed, fought, wept, fell in and out of love, revealed their darkest secrets in preposterous dream ballets, and, as the second act reached the forty-five-minute mark, resolved every conflict in an improbably swift series of coincidences that necessitated reprise performances of several songs the audience had already heard. And the audience laughed and wept right along.

How could that be? Philip was a person who liked to understand things, and he had thought long and hard about this. The conclusion he came to was that the realness of *Aurora*— and by extension, of all musicals—did not exist despite the singing and dancing, but because of it.

After all, the characters in *Aurora* expressed themselves far more fully than anyone who didn't launch into a musical number at every strong emotion ever could. If Philip himself could feel half as real and alive as those made-up characters who lived on the stage of the Rialto Theatre for two hours at a time, eight times a week—well, that would be an excellent feeling indeed.

Philip and Emily had taken their seats. The houselights started to dim.

"Cell phone?" he whispered to Emily. It was a ritual of theirs, because one time she'd forgotten and of course it had rung right in the middle of the quietest song in the show.

She'd been so upset afterward that Philip had promised her he would never, ever forget to remind her to turn her phone off before the show started, and he never had.

"Got it," whispered Emily as she pressed the Off button and dropped the phone back into her bag. She squeezed his leg in anticipation.

Houselights faded to black. The conductor brought down his baton with enough vigor to slice a watermelon in half, and that very instant the theatre was filled with the music they loved so much.

Performance number 1,014 of *Aurora* had begun.

3

"DON'T RAIN ON MY PARADE"

Funny Girl
1964. Music by Jule Styne, lyrics by Bob Merrill,
book by Isobel Lennart

In addition to his spreadsheets, Philip also kept a notebook in which he jotted various facts and figures about *Aurora*. For example: backstage at every performance were one stage manager and three assistant stage managers, one of whom doubled as the dance captain. There were twenty-five union stagehands, two follow-spot operators, and a "sound guy." The show could not be performed without these people, but the audience never even saw them.

The notebook had a separate tabbed section labeled "Critical Theories." These were varied and contradictory, including:

1. *Aurora* represented an innovative step forward in the hybrid Broadway pop-rock musical

(*Hair, Jesus Christ Superstar, Tommy, Rent,* and a few others defined this admittedly skimpy tradition).

2. *Aurora* pandered to a naïve audience hungry for melodrama and *American Idol*–style screeching (an irritating theory born of cynicism and envy, in Philip's opinion).

3. The show would never have succeeded without the incandescent performance of its star, Marlena Ortiz, and would fail as soon as she left.

4. *Aurora* was fresh and perhaps flawed yet undeniably "worked," as proven by its loyal fan base and generally strong ticket sales.

The entire back third of Philip's notebook was devoted to "The Mystery": namely, the fact that nobody—except, as Philip would be careful to say, the person or people who had done it—knew who had written *Aurora*.

The anonymity of *Aurora*'s author had been considered a shameless marketing gimmick when the show first opened on Broadway. Everyone in the industry thought it was a ploy, and that the true identity of the creator or creators of this smash hit would be revealed in some kind of follow-up publicity stunt. But he, she, or they never were.

And when *Aurora* won the Tony Award for Best Book and Best Original Score, and the director breathlessly accepted the gleaming statuettes "on behalf of Aurora, the *real* Aurora, who chooses to remain anonymous," and then broke down in sobs at the podium on national television, that's when it became clear that this was no ploy. Someone had written the smash hit of the season, and whoever it was did not want anyone to know his, her, or their identity. It was Broadway's best-kept and most gossiped-about secret.

"Emily, could you see me after class?"

Mr. Henderson did not sound pleased.

After Emily's last two papers for Mr. Henderson's English composition class, she had been firmly instructed that she could write about any subject under the sun except *Aurora*. One of her papers had been on the use of flight imagery in *Aurora*'s lyrics; the other, more fantastic story depicted in detail a dream Emily had had, in which Marlena Ortiz showed up at school in her *Aurora* costume and revealed herself to the entire student body to be Emily's best, best friend. Then she and Emily sang a duet on stage at the sophomore spring dance and brought down the house.

Did a tiny part of Emily's brain know that her persuasive essay about who had really written *Aurora* was the literary equivalent of flipping Mr. Henderson the bird? Perhaps, but she'd convinced herself otherwise. Not until this instant, as she took the long, ominous walk from her desk to his, did it occur to her that she might have been wrong about that.

If my life were a musical, Emily thought, trying to bolster her confidence as she waited for her teacher to be done answering last-minute questions from a few stragglers, *this would be one of those times where I sang a big defiant song that told everyone to shut up. Like "Don't Rain on My Parade,"* she decided. Just thinking of Barbra Streisand belting out her big number from *Funny Girl* made Emily stand a little taller.

Now all her classmates had gone. She saw her persuasive essay on Mr. Henderson's desk. There was plenty of red scribble on it, but she couldn't see if there was a grade.

"Emily," he said, peering up at her over his glasses. "What happened? I thought we agreed you were going to broaden your horizons."

"I did," she said. "It's not about *Aurora*. It's about the mystery of who wrote *Aurora*." Somehow the logic of this sounded better in her head than when she said it out loud, but she stuck to her guns. "Didn't you get that?"

"Emily, Emily, Emily," he sighed. "I cannot accept this paper." He stood up, and Emily was reminded of how short Barbra Streisand was in real life. "I want you to write a persuasive essay about something else. Not *Aurora* the show, not *Aurora* the person. I don't want you to write about the aurora borealis!"

Very witty, Emily thought. Mr. Henderson looked crabby all of a sudden, which made her wonder if she'd rolled her eyes by accident.

"I want you to write a persuasive essay that does not have the word 'aurora' in it *at all*." Students for the next period were already wandering into the classroom, and Mr. Henderson sounded impatient. "Okay? I won't mark it late if you give it to me by Monday."

Emily shifted her weight from foot to foot and tried to think of a rebuttal. "But now I have to do two papers and everyone else just did one," she said finally. "That's not fair!"

"Sure it is," he replied. He picked up the eraser and started to clean the blackboard for his next class. "I'm encouraging you to find other interests. Enlarge your perspective. Read the newspaper, for heaven's sake!"

"But, Mr. Henderson!" Emily protested. "You're raining on my parade!"

"You're a big girl, Emily," Mr. Henderson said, ending the

conversation. "You knew what you were doing when you wrote this. Don't make me send a note home."

"You don't have to do that," she said in a rush. "I'll have a new essay for you on Monday."

"And?"

Emily bit her lip. "I won't mention *Aurora*."

Emily's parents liked the theatre well enough, but her grandma Rose had a passion for it. Grandma Rose was Mr. Pearl's mother and she lived downstairs, with her own bedroom and bathroom on the lower level of the Pearls' modest split-level home in Rockville Centre.

In her younger days, Grandma Rose had been a music teacher, and it was largely thanks to her that Emily had acquired a love of Broadway musicals at an early age. *Fiddler on the Roof* was Grandma Rose's all-time favorite, but she'd also introduced Emily to *Annie* (of course) and many others. *The Phantom of the Opera. Cats. Into the Woods. Beauty and the Beast. The Lion King* (that was a special outing that had also included Mr. Pearl, who normally stuck with serious, preferably British plays that had been recast with famous American film actors).

Due to Grandma Rose's influence, watching the Tony Awards broadcast on television was an annual Pearl family ritual, complete with specially prepared snacks and glasses of inexpensive champagne, from which even Emily was allowed a celebratory sip. Last year Philip had been invited to join them. It had been a marvelous evening, almost too marvelous for Philip to bear. Parents who liked each other! Laughter in the living room! Home-cooked snacks—and the Tony Awards! It was a lot to absorb.

Mrs. Pearl found Emily's attachment to *Aurora* amusing, a phase, "a typical teenage thing" (she was the one who provided Hanukkah-present indulgences like Emily's *Aurora* messenger bag). However, Mr. Pearl thought Emily's fascination with "that show" was obsessive. He often warned Emily that if her grades started to slip, he would be taking "a close look at how you spend your time, young lady."

This was why a note home from Mr. Henderson would be most unwelcome, from Emily's perspective. Especially a note that said she was too interested in *Aurora*. That was all her father needed to hear.

4

"GOODNIGHT"

I Do! I Do!
1966. Music by Harvey Schmidt, lyrics and
book by Tom Jones

BwayPhil: Still awake?
AURORAROX: yez,
AURORAROX: mr henderson said to read the newspaper
AURORAROX: so i am
AURORAROX: did you know
AURORAROX: there are all these sections of the Times
AURORAROX: that are not the Arts and Leisure section?
BwayPhil: I had heard of that, yes.
AURORAROX: i don't understand the news at all
AURORAROX: i think it's like one of those complicated tv series
AURORAROX: where you have to watch from the beginning
AURORAROX: or you can't follow what's going on
AURORAROX: so what are you doing?

BwayPhil: nuthin

AURORAROX: i know that nuthin

AURORAROX: something wrong?

BwayPhil: Nah. Just—ok, I'll give you a clue. Show question:

BwayPhil: "My world's coming unwrapped"

BwayPhil: What musical is that from?

BwayPhil: Hint—it's based on Shakespeare.

AURORAROX: Kiss Me, Kate?

BwayPhil: Nope.

AURORAROX: well it's not West Side Story

BwayPhil: I admit, it's very obscure.

AURORAROX: forget it then! I give up

BwayPhil: "My world's coming unwrapped," from *Oh, Brother!* Loosely based on *The Comedy of Errors*. 1981, music by Michael Valenti, book and lyrics by Donald Driver. Big flop! Closed after 13 previews and 3 perfs.

BwayPhil: The clue is the title, btw.

AURORAROX: oh, brother

AURORAROX: oh! Mark?

AURORAROX: what'd he do now?

BwayPhil: Just acting like his usual disgusting self when I got in.

AURORAROX: ignore, ignore

BwayPhil: I do, I do!

BwayPhil: Now there's a nice name for a musical!

AURORAROX: :-P

AURORAROX: put on some music & tune out the world

AURORAROX: that's what I'm going to do now

AURORAROX: this newspaper thing is bogus

AURORAROX: ooh, Marlena's singing "Never Be Enough"

BwayPhil: First act version or second act reprise?

AURORAROX: first act.

AURORAROX: i'll hold my headphones to the screen
AURORAROX: so you can hear
BwayPhil: Funny.
BwayPhil: Hey, I ***can*** hear it.
AURORAROX: course you can, listen—

> *"forever will have to be enough,*
> *not one day less will do,*
> *But forever will never be enough*
> *to celebrate*
> *alllllll*
> *myyyyyyyy*
> *looooooooooove—"*

BwayPhil: "for yooooooooou!!!!!"
AURORAROX: *thunderous applause*
BwayPhil: It's Wednesday.
AURORAROX: they did the show twice today
BwayPhil: Sometimes I hate that they do it without us.
AURORAROX: me too
AURORAROX: but we will be there again soon
AURORAROX: sleep tight now
BwayPhil: Night, Em—thanks for the song.
AURORAROX: don't thank me
AURORAROX: thank whoever
AURORAROX: thank Aurora
BwayPhil: Okay I will.
BwayPhil: Thank you Aurora, whoever you are!

5

"THE TELEPHONE HOUR"

Bye Bye Birdie
1960. Music by Charles Strouse, lyrics by Lee Adams,
book by Michael Stewart

Although Emily and Philip always called it Philip's house (as in, "See you later, Mom, I'm going to spend Saturday prepping for the PSAT at Philip's house"—sometimes little white lies like this were necessary to explain what it was exactly the two of them did together every Saturday), the term "Philip's house" was not technically accurate. Unlike most of the kids he knew, Philip and his brother, Mark, and their mother, when she was around, lived in an apartment, not a house. A "garden apartment," it was called, in a complex called Birchwood Gardens.

But there were no gardens, nothing that bloomed or smelled good or was nice to look at. The main geographic feature was a long, snaky parking lot that meandered like an asphalt stream around all the separate buildings of Birchwood

Gardens, providing each apartment with two of its very own parking spots, *whoop-de-doo*. Like Philip would ever have his own car.

Philip's family had one of the upstairs apartments in D building, which was really a pair of attached duplex town homes. "Fastest gun in D-West!" Mark would joke, when he was acting stupid. That was pretty often.

Mark was nineteen and enrolled in community college in alleged pursuit of a business degree, but he rarely attended classes. He liked to play video games, chase girls, and hang out with his equally boneheaded friends. Sometimes he did these things at his friends' houses, but often they came over to Birchwood Gardens, apartment D-West, since Mrs. Nebbling was rarely home.

Not that Philip's mother was a bad parent; at least, Philip didn't think she was. She had a solid track record of being a perfectly adequate and occasionally standout mother (home-made Halloween costumes were a particular strength, though Philip was too old for that now). She'd been home practically all the time when Philip and Mark were young.

But that was before the divorce. Now, after three years of heroic effort, she'd finally passed the bar exam and gotten a job as an actual lawyer. She was making decent money, but three years of living off credit cards, student loans, and part-time jobs had dug a pretty deep hole for the remnants of the Nebbling family to climb out of. Nevertheless, Mrs. Nebbling refused to let Mark get a job until he finished school.

"It's bad enough I had to work my way through college," she would say when Mark batted his bleary eyes and sweetly offered to drop out and apply for a graveyard shift at the local Dunkin' Donuts, precisely because he knew she would never allow it. "You boys are going to have an easier time of it."

Of course, Philip would think bitterly, *she has no idea just how easy a time Mark is having.* That was because Mrs. Nebbling spent days at a time at the AllChem industrial storage facility in Wilmington, Delaware, wearing a hazmat suit and shouting questions through her mask to similarly dressed employees of AllChem. Some very nasty stuff had been dumped in the Delaware River, apparently. Now there was a lawsuit. Mrs. Nebbling's firm represented AllChem, and her task was taking depositions.

If my life were a musical, Philip sometimes thought, *there would be a song called "Allied Chemical versus the State of Delaware."* It would start with twenty dancers dressed in hazmat suits, which they would soon tear off to reveal the spangled leotards underneath. The final chorus would have the dancers tapping and splashing their way through vats of noxious chemical goo.

Sort of like "Singin' in the Rain," he would think. *Only carcinogenic.*

Mark was far from an ideal big brother, but this didn't mean he paid no attention to Philip. Quite the contrary: Mark had made it his personal mission to hound Philip into admitting that he was gay.

"Look around you, dude. There's just a lot of queer-type crap in this room, you know?" This was the conversation that made Philip later complain to Emily about Mark being a jerk.

"They're *Playbills,* you idiot. I collect them. They could be valuable someday," Philip added, though he wasn't really sure about this.

Mark shrugged. "I'm just saying—you're not showing a normal interest in girls."

"But I don't like boys, either."

"That's because you're latent," explained Mark, patiently feeding a fresh supply of fake IDs through the laminating machine he kept stashed under his bed. He sold these for a tidy profit. In most areas of his life Mark was lazy and dishonest, but when it came to his antisocial pursuits he was nothing short of entrepreneurial. "You're gay, dude. You just don't know it yet."

Philip found this kind of logic hard to refute, but talking to Mark was a waste of time anyway, so he didn't bother to try.

"Look who it is! Hey, guys! Are you seeing a show today? We're seeing *Mamma Mia!* Oh my God! We heard it was great. Have you seen it? Was it great?"

Five squealing girls from Eleanor Roosevelt High School had boarded the same Long Island Rail Road car as Emily and Philip and plopped themselves in the seats directly across the aisle. Now they would all be together for the full thirty-eight-minute ride.

Emily knew their names. Michelle, Cindy, Chantal, Lorelei, and Beth. She'd had classes with some of them last year, and Beth was in the same period of Mr. Henderson's English comp class.

How did we not see them on the platform? thought Emily. *We could have ducked into another car. Now I have to listen to them go on and on and on—*

"First we're going to go shopping at H&M! And then we're having lunch at Planet Hollywood. And then we're going to the show. It's at, um, three?"

"Saturday and Wednesday matinees are at two," said Philip dryly. "Sunday matinees are at three."

"Well, that's confusing!" said Cindy.

"It's because the actors have another show to do at eight on Wednesdays and Saturdays, and they have to have a dinner break." Philip explained. "It's a union rule."

Michelle smiled and tossed her hair. "Okay, so then we're seeing *Mamma Mia!* at two. And then if we really really love it, which we will because I hear it's great, we thought we would go to Virgin and get the soundtrack CD."

"You mean cast album," said Emily, trying not to sneer. "Soundtracks are from movies. Shows have cast albums."

"Same thing!" giggled Michelle. "And then we're getting pedicures! Because it doesn't have to be summer to have pretty feet, right?"

"Pedicures, pedicures, pedicures!" Cindy and Chantal and Lorelei and Beth chirped in unison. Well, not really, but that's what it seemed like in Emily's head. Like they were starting a chirping, squealing musical number, like the one from *Bye Bye Birdie* where all the teenagers go crazy because some big singing star is coming to town. It was called "The Telephone Hour"; Philip had played it for her once.

"Spring! Oh my God!" Cindy shrieked. "Did you hear? Evelyn told me that Frankie Russo told her that Mr. Henderson told him what the spring musical is going to be!"

Chantal and Lorelei and Beth and Michelle started bouncing up and down on the seats. "What what what what what?"

Cindy frowned. "She said it was going to be *Fiddler on the Roof.*"

A collective, disappointed sigh escaped the girls.

"A classic," said Philip. "One of the best shows ever." Emily nodded in agreement.

"Yes, but the *costumes*," Chantal moaned. "Aren't the characters, like, peasants?"

"I guess we won't be driving the football team wild with our Hot Box Girls costumes this year!" Lorelei quipped.

At that, the five girls started spontaneously singing "A Bushel and a Peck" from *Guys and Dolls* in their highest, squeakiest voices.

Emily slumped in her seat and hid behind her Week in Review section from last Sunday's *Times*, which so far had not provided any inspiration for her persuasive essay, other than to argue that newspaper ink should be made less smudgy. And Philip wished he'd brought some aspirin. Didn't these girls realize how idiotic they were? He'd seen them in *Guys and Dolls* last year, out of morbid curiosity. The band had sounded like— well, like a high school band. The voices were uneven. The dancing, embarrassing. The acting ranged from soap opera to nonexistent. And those tacky, sequined, far-too-revealing Hot Box Girls costumes—the stuff of nightmares! On Broadway, at least, if you were wearing a skimpy costume, it was because you actually had a great body. In high school, this was not always the case.

"Hey, Emily!" said Beth. "Mr. Henderson is always saying how you're some kind of theatre fanatic. How come you guys don't try out for the shows?"

Because you are deluded, Emily wanted to say. *Because we know people who are trained actors, who are on Broadway, who are actually talented—who carry on like fools just like you do, but they've earned the right because they are really good at what they do!*

What she said was, "Because they su—"

"We prefer," Philip said, carefully interrupting Emily before she finished the last word, "the *professional* theatre."

"Huh," said Michelle. "Whatever. So what show are you seeing today?"

Emily smiled. *"Aurora."* The word itself made her happy.

"Aurora." Michelle's face looked semiblank but her voice maintained its high-pitched, overexcited tone. "Awesome! I haven't seen that but I hear it's great! Oh my God, have you seen *Avenue Q*? Have you seen *Wicked*?"

The other girls started chattering.

"I totally saw *Wicked*! It was great!"

"I thought *Phantom* was great, too!"

"I hear the food at Planet Hollywood is great."

"Our *Mamma Mia!* seats are really great!" added Cindy. "My mom bought the tickets. She said we were in the downstairs part."

"You mean the orchestra section?" Philip said.

"Oh my God, I *hope* we're not sitting with the band!" Cindy pretended to faint and the other girls giggled. "Though if we're going to meet some cute musicians, maybe we should get our pedicures first!"

Then they kicked off their shoes to compare feet, each one claiming hers were the *absolute worst*. Soon there were ten girlish legs waving around in the air, like the June Taylor Dancers.

Not that they'd know who the June Taylor Dancers were, thought Philip. He looked over at Emily to catch her eye and share a moment of "Can you believe these dum-dums?" but Emily had propped her head against the window in despair and her eyes were closed.

Philip glanced back at the giggling centipede and decided to follow Emily's lead. *Thank God for* Fiddler, he thought, leaning back in his seat. *Put these five in some ankle-length peasant dresses, quick.*

6

"DIAMONDS ARE A GIRL'S BEST FRIEND"

Gentlemen Prefer Blondes
1949. Music by Jule Styne, lyrics by Leo Robin,
book by Joseph Fields and Anita Loos

As she and Philip walked from the Rialto Theatre to the Café Edison for their prematinee lunch date with Ian and Stephanie Dawson (their precious *Aurora* rush tickets had already been purchased and tucked into Philip's backpack), Emily added up the expenses that would be incurred that day by the five-headed, shrieking spending machine that was Michelle, Cindy, Chantal, Lorelei, and Beth.

A hundred dollars each for orchestra seats to *Mamma Mia!*

Twenty-five dollars, easy, for lunch in that overpriced tourist trap.

A trip to the Virgin Megastore to buy "soundtracks" (duh): another twenty-five dollars each.

Pedicures? Who knew? Twenty dollars, Emily figured.

Shopping? At least fifty dollars each, maybe more.

Plus the fourteen-dollar round-trip train fare from Rockville Centre to Penn Station. And these girls would probably take taxis everywhere.

Conservatively, then, each one of those squealing dimwits would be spending close to two hundred fifty dollars today.

Two hundred and fifty dollars each! One thousand, two hundred and fifty dollars total!

That was fifty discount rush tickets to *Aurora*. Practically a year's worth.

Thank goodness for Grandma Rose, Emily thought, and she resolved to spend no more than seven dollars at the Edison: that would cover a cup of soup, tax, and tip. She was craving a cheeseburger, but unlike Michelle, Cindy, Chantal, Lorelei, and Beth, Emily was on a budget.

The very first time Emily had seen *Aurora*, it was her father's brother, crazy Uncle David, who'd given her the tickets. Emily was thirteen at the time and too young to go by herself, so Grandma Rose had taken her.

It was a fateful night, for her and for Philip as well—really, what were the odds of both of them being there at the first preview of a new musical hardly anyone had heard of? It only took one performance to forge their special, permanent bond—a bond as indelible as an autograph signed in the bold black ink of a Sharpie. . . .

"Who is this Marlena Ortiz?" Grandma Rose had said as they gathered up their coats. The show was over and everyone was leaving, but young Emily, tears still wet on her cheeks, was frozen in her seat, staring at the empty stage. "Marlena Ortiz, she's all right," Grandma Rose decided. "No Ethel Merman, but cute. So, what did you think? Did you like it? I thought it was pretty loud. But that's what the public goes for these days. Come on, darling, people want to get out."

Grandma Rose kept chatting as Emily stood up like a sleepwalker and allowed herself to be led out of the theatre. In her head it was all still going on. The story. The music. The dancing. Emily had seen a lot of Broadway shows, maybe even more than most girls from theatre-happy families in the New York metropolitan area, but she had never seen anything that touched her like this.

> *Never be enough,*
> *My love for you could never be enough,*
> *Ten thousand years could never be enough*
> *To say what's in my heart—*

"Come on, let's get her autograph!" said Grandma Rose, waving the souvenir program she'd purchased for Emily. "Who knows, that Marlena Ortiz, maybe she'll be a big star someday."

Emily and her grandmother pushed their way through the chattering mob outside the theatre. The air tingled with the collective excitement of 1,545 people who'd just been the first human beings on the planet to see a new Broadway musical: one that had the rare, intoxicating smell of a hit.

The stage door of the Rialto was on the side of the theatre, down a short alley. The crowd waiting there numbered at least thirty and seemed to be mostly pros—professional autograph hounds who'd already amassed stacks of first-night *Playbills*, with Sharpie markers at the ready to thrust at whichever actor emerged first.

"I know him," Emily blurted out. One of the people in the front of the crowd, nearest the stage door, looked really familiar. In fact, she was sure he went to her school.

"Philip, right?" she called over the din. "Philip?" She had to call again even louder, because the stage door had opened and everyone was screaming. But it was one of the musicians, dressed all in black and grinning with embarrassment that he wasn't who the crowd wanted. *"Philip Nebbling?"*

Finally hearing his name, Philip turned around. Thirteen years old but looking older because he was tall for his age, even skinnier than he'd be a few years later, eyes rimmed red from crying through the last twenty minutes of the show—Philip Nebbling had run off to the city by himself that night because he couldn't bear to stay home and face what he'd just found out. ("A garlic farm?" he'd screamed at his mother as she'd tried to explain, the phone still in her hand. *He'd lost his father to a woman with a garlic farm?*)

Now the show was over and he was standing at the stage door, waiting for what exactly he wasn't sure. All he knew was that the worst day of his life had turned, improbably, into the best, and he wanted, he *needed* the magic of this night to last a few minutes longer. And now somebody was calling his name.

From the expression on his face when he finally looked up and saw Emily calling to him, Emily could tell they were about to become best, best friends.

Aurora.

He got it, too.

Afterward she and Philip had had to make do with only occasional visits to the show, funded at first by Emily's accumulated birthday and Hanukkah money and later by Grandma Rose's generosity. Unlike Emily's parents, Grandma Rose didn't need to be convinced that seeing the same show over and over again was a valid expense.

"When your father was a baby," Grandma Rose liked to recount to Emily at the dinner table, "once a week I left him with my sister for the afternoon, and you know what I did? I saw *Fiddler on the Roof*! Every Wednesday afternoon! With Zero Mostel, every Wednesday!"

Mrs. Pearl would ladle more mashed potatoes onto everyone's plates in an attempt to change the subject, but Grandma Rose was tenacious. "What a performance!" she would crow, gesturing with her fork. "So sad! So funny! So *true*!" Then she would sing: "If I were a rich man! Ya-hah-deedle-deedle-bubba-bubba-deedle-deedle-dum!"

Of course, when Zero Mostel starred in the original Broadway production of *Fiddler*, it was 1964 and a balcony seat for a Saturday matinee of a Broadway musical cost three dollars and sixty cents. Mere latte money! Emily found the figure impossible to believe, until Grandma Rose showed her the old *Fiddler* ticket stubs and *Playbills* in her scrapbook.

It wasn't until Emily turned fifteen and was allowed to go into Manhattan without an adult ("As long as you travel with a friend," her parents had stipulated, "and stay together the whole time") that seeing *Aurora* on a weekly basis became a possibility. But even at the rush-line price of twenty-five dollars a ticket, two people seeing the show every Saturday quickly added up to a significant sum. There was also the round-trip train fare to the city and lunch at the Edison to pay for.

That was when Emily struck her deal. Now, Grandma

Rose had made it clear she didn't have unlimited funds, and she had a slew of grandnephews and grandnieces to spoil. So the secret weekly *Aurora* allowance she provided was not an outright gift, but a loan—or, as they called it in show business, an *advance.*

"Don't worry, you've got it," Grandma Rose would say as she counted out the tens and twenties every week, enough to cover both Emily and Philip's expenses (of course Emily paid for Philip; she had to, because they were best friends and fellow Aurorafans and he was poor). "You've got money in the bank, darling," Grandma Rose assured her. "From your bat mitzvah. You'll pay me back when you're older."

Grandma kept her cash in a cigar box in her top dresser drawer, and Emily always tried to catch a glimpse of what else was in there when Grandma tucked the box away. She could have sworn she'd once seen a label from Victoria's Secret, which was an odd feeling. Grandma was seventy-five, after all.

Anyway, this week, like every other week, Emily had thanked her grandmother profusely for the loan.

Grandma shrugged. "What if I'd waited to see Zero Mostel? Now he's dead. And they didn't even use him in the movie! They used that other man, the one with the strange name."

"Topol." Emily didn't find Topol any stranger a name than Zero, but Grandma was entitled to her opinion. "He was good, Grandma. He got nominated for the Academy Award."

"He's no Zero Mostel, that's all I'm saying. Now, *that* was a Tevye." Grandma Rose's whole face crinkled when she smiled. "This is my point, darling. You have to see your show while it's running. 'Cause when it's over—goodbye, Charlie. That's my advice." And she grabbed Emily by the earlobe and gave a little pinch, and that was that.

★   ★   ★

"So who is this 'SAVEMEFROMAURORA' jerk?" said Stephanie, slurping a soy milk smoothie. Actors had to be at the theatre by half hour to get into makeup and costume (that meant one-thirty for a two o'clock matinee), so Stephanie could only briefly grace the Edison with her presence.

Ian snorted. "Have you crossed paths with that bozo, too? He's haunting all the chat rooms, bad-mouthing the show and pissing everyone off."

"What a completely *toxic* person!" said Stephanie, shaking her wavy carrot-colored tresses around like a wet dog. "He's even been leaving nasty posts on the show's message boards. 'Abandon hope, all ye who enter here!' *Such* crap. I mean, 'ye'? Who talks like that?"

"We chatted with him once," Emily piped up. She was glad to have something to contribute. "What a loser."

"I think he's a publicist for *Wicked*," Ian said. Stephanie screamed and slapped her hand over Ian's mouth. Every head in the Edison turned.

"Don't say things like that, Ian," she scolded. "That's how rumors start. Especially in *this* place!"

She was right about the rumors. Tucked in the lobby of the Edison Hotel, the Café Edison had been a Broadway performers' hangout since the 1930s. There were long-legged gypsies at every table, swaying like palm trees in the breeze as they leaned in to gossip and out to eavesdrop; in, out, rinse and repeat.

"I'm sure that SAVEME is just a crank," said Philip, gently dabbing his lips with a napkin. "He does seem to know his musicals pretty well."

"Not as well as you, darling!" Stephanie giggled. "You are an *encyclopedia*! Men with brains are so sexy. No wonder Ian chose you as the object of his affections, of all the nubile young boys on the rush line!"

At this, Ian collapsed and pounded his forehead dramatically on the table, almost knocking over everyone's water. Philip looked like a deer caught in a follow-spot. Emily felt her face flush with embarrassment, but on whose behalf she wasn't sure.

"You're such a troublemaker, Dawson!" Ian moaned. "Young Philip here, though admittedly pretty as a chorus girl and sharp as Ben Brantley's tongue, is *not* my boyfriend."

"Well, not *yet!*" Stephanie chirped. But something about the look on Philip's and Emily's faces finally activated her shut-up mechanism. "I'm sorry, that was rude. I shouldn't assume things, right?" She slurped the last of her smoothie. "It's just that at LaGuardia, people are, like, *flinging* themselves out of the closet all freshman year, so I just thought . . . Oh, my, I'm digging myself in deeper and deeper, aren't I!" Her laugh trickled up and down the scale like a vocal exercise.

"Darling, our young friends are not *from* here," said Ian. "They're from—not Kansas, but someplace similar, no?"

"Rockville Centre," Emily said, feeling like a rube. (One of the ways Emily and Philip had first known they would be friends forever was when they'd simultaneously observed that the name of their hometown was spelled with an "re" at the end. "Just like theatre!" they'd said in awe, at exactly the same time. To Emily it felt like fate. To Philip, it was kismet. "*Kismet*, 1953," he'd explained with reverence. "Book by Charles Lederer and Luther Davis, music and lyrics by Robert Wright and George Forrest, adapted from the music of Alexander Borodin.")

Ian continued berating Stephanie. "Yes, Rockville Cen-

treeeeee. So use some discretion, you little tart. Anyway, I have something much more interesting to talk about than who is and who isn't! Guess what I know?"

Stephanie glanced at her watch. "Make it quick, I have to get to the theatre."

"Oh, I'm not speeding through this story. It's too good," Ian purred cruelly. "It's the best gossip ever!"

"Tell me, suckface! I have to go!"

"Well, it's a long saga. . . . To do it justice, one would have to go all the way back to the beginning . . . to when the Greeks invented theatre, and the first leather-clad thespians lithped acroth the thtage. . . ." Ian dodged Stephanie's barrage of slaps. Emily was finding it hard to keep up, and Philip had taken himself out of the line of fire by busying himself with the check.

"Ian, you are the *worst*! I can't be late for half hour again, the stage manager will have me over his knee."

"You'd better go then, Spanky," he said, laughing and batting her hands away. "I'll tell you later. Or maybe I won't! It can be your punishment for being rude to my friends."

Calmly, Stephanie stood up and plopped a big juicy kiss on Philip's mouth. When she was done, she glared at Ian. "Fine. Philip is *mine*, then. That's *your* punishment. Because you," she said, turning back to Philip, "are *not* in Kansas anymore."

Stephanie threw a few dollars on the table and hustled out the door, already late. The faster she moved, the more evident her dancer's waddle became, her slim legs permanently turned out, ducklike, from hour after hour, year after year of doing pliés in front of a mirror.

Emily was too flustered by Stephanie's smooch attack to

speak. It was Philip, managing to remain perfectly composed despite the big scarlet lip print on the lower portion of his face, who finally asked: "So what is this gossip, Ian?"

Ian looked quite serious all of a sudden. He leaned close to them and whispered, "I know who wrote *Aurora*."

7

"DON'T CRY FOR ME, ARGENTINA"

Evita
**1979. Music by Andrew Lloyd Webber,
lyrics and book by Tim Rice**

Even Ian's tiny whisper caused a palpable hush to fall across the Café Edison, and he refused to say another word until, as he said, "we have entered a secure undisclosed location." Emily decided the second row of the far right mezzanine of the Rialto Theatre was secure enough. As soon as Philip returned from the men's room (the lipstick was gone when he came out) and they took their seats for the matinee, she pounced.

"Okay. No *way*," She felt ready to start slapping Ian herself. "There is no way you can know what you said you know."

"Shhhh!" Ian hissed dramatically. "Someone I met in Florida told me. But only because I swore not to tell."

"How's that going so far, by the way?" Philip had to fold his long legs like a crane's to fit in the narrow row of seats. "The not telling part, I mean."

"I *haven't* told, have I, Miss Smug Thing?" Ian shot back. "And the way you're behaving, maybe I won't."

"Ian! You would never have mentioned it if you didn't mean to tell us." Emily smiled sweetly. "You're not *that* much of a jerk!"

"No matter what people say," added Philip. Ian started to laugh. They had him.

"C'mon, we'll swear, too," Emily cajoled. "Not to tell *and* not to tell anyone we know something we can't tell them." Emily was on fire to know, for all the obvious reasons, of course, but also because if there was a chance she'd been right in her persuasive essay, she was going to march into Mr. Henderson's class on Monday and make a scene. Of course, if she swore not to repeat what Ian told her, she wouldn't be able to say *why* she was making a scene, and Mr. Henderson would think she was losing her mind, but still . . .

"Did this Florida person say how he, she, or it found out?" Philip asked as they all half stood to let a latecomer take her seat at the end of the row. "Because maybe, dear gullible Ian, your leg has been pulled."

They lowered themselves back into their seats, and Ian spoke in an intense stage whisper. "The 'Florida person' has an impeccable inside track on such information. He, she, or it was utterly shocked with what he, she, or it was unexpectedly made privy to!"

Pronouns suck, thought Emily. *Just spit it out, the show's about to start*. And it was. Like a flock of geese whose group mind mysteriously knew how to find South America, the whole audience went quiet a split second before the house-lights started to dim.

"Cell phone?" Even under these highly distracting conditions Philip didn't forget. Emily fished through her bag frantically to find the phone.

"I will tell you this," Ian said as the houselights came down for performance number 1,022 of *Aurora*. "It's somebody *famous*."

★   ★   ★

> *Never be enough,*
> *My love for you could*
> *Never be enough.*
> *Infinity could never be enough*
> *To hold what's in my heart.*
> *I'll stay with you when times are tough,*
> *We'll never be apart—*
>
> *Never understand,*
> *The rest of them will*
> *Never understand.*
> *A love so far beyond*
> *The love that we had planned . . .*

AURORAROX: so who do you think?

AURORAROX: someone famous, now.

BwayPhil: ugh! Impossible, AURORA just doesn't sound like anyone else.

AURORAROX: Sondheim?

BwayPhil: Emily, be serious—he wrote Sweeney Todd! He wrote Into the Woods! And Company, and Sunday in the Park with George, and Pacific Overtures and A Little Night Music and and and . . .

AURORAROX: i know what he wrote!

BwayPhil: I would hear half a bar of Sondheim coming a mile away!

AURORAROX: i was just starting with famous

AURORAROX: Andrew Lloyd Webber?

BwayPhil: Absolutely not.

AURORAROX: Richard Rodgers?

BwayPhil: Famous and ***alive***, I think would also be important.

AURORAROX: duh. that shrinks the list somewhat

AURORAROX: Elton John? Stephen Schwartz? William Finn?

BwayPhil: William Finn is not really famous.

AURORAROX: we know who he is

AURORAROX: he wrote Spelling Bee

AURORAROX: he wrote Falsettos

BwayPhil: He's famous to the people who know who he is. That's not the same as being famous. Anyway, the songs from Aurora don't sound like any of them.

BwayPhil: Or anybody else I've ever heard.

BwayPhil: That's why I love them.

AURORAROX: i know!

AURORAROX: "Never Be Enough" is just the best song

AURORAROX: ever

SAVEMEFROMAURORA: looky, ma, the kids are playing "who wrote Aurora?"

SAVEMEFROMAURORA: I'm more of a Scrabble fan myself.

AURORAROX: oh no

AURORAROX: it's back

SAVEMEFROMAURORA: Hush! Now listen: "The best song ever." That simply cannot be true, and I want you to admit it.

AURORAROX: but it IS.

SAVEMEFROMAURORA: You think it's better than "Somewhere over the Rainbow." Better than "Hey Jude." Better than pretty much anything from Gypsy or Oklahoma! or My Fair Lady?

BwayPhil: Why don't you go ***see*** the show and come back and apologize for your ignorance?

SAVEMEFROMAURORA: What makes you think I haven't seen it?

AURORAROX: because if you had SEEN it

AURORAROX: we would not be having

AURORAROX: this conversation.

SAVEMEFROMAURORA: I've seen it.

AURORAROX: see it

AURORAROX: until you GET it

SAVEMEFROMAURORA: Trust me, I've seen it more than you.

AURORAROX: LOL!!!!! no way.

BwayPhil: Wait—do we know you?

BwayPhil: Are you that crabby guy who's always on the rush line in a Jekyll & Hyde show jacket?

SAVEMEFROMAURORA: J&H ! ! ! ! horrors!

AURORAROX: OMG, if you're a regular

AURORAROX: we must totally know you

SAVEMEFROMAURORA: "Have I said too much?"

BwayPhil: "Don't Cry for Me, Argentina," Evita. 1979. Andrew Lloyd Webber and Tim Rice.

SAVEMEFROMAURORA: "There's nothing more I can think of to say to you."

AURORAROX: So who are you, SAVEME?

BwayPhil: yoo-hoo! SAVEME?

AURORAROX: he logged off.

BwayPhil: Weird.

★   ★   ★

Why Broadway Shows Should Be Free
A Persuasive Essay by Emily Pearl

Emily gritted her teeth as Mr. Henderson read her essay, right there in front of her, as the rest of the students noisily exited the classroom.

Yes, her paper was about Broadway. But it didn't mention *Aurora,* not even once. Instead she used *Fiddler* (the original 1964 production, starring Zero Mostel, of course) and *The Lion King* as her examples, and had even prepared a small bar chart titled "Broadway Ticket Prices, Then and Now." A chart! What could be more persuasive than that? The use of infographics was the one good idea she'd picked up from reading the *Times,* and she was half expecting a generous helping of extra credit for her efforts.

Mr. Henderson clucked his tongue against the roof of his mouth. "Emily Pearl," he said. "What am I going to do with you?"

"It doesn't mention *Aurora,*" Emily said. "Did you see I made a chart?"

"It doesn't, and you did. Very impressive. Broadway tickets are much more expensive than they used to be. I get it." He took off his glasses and laid them on her paper. "That is what we call self-evident, Emily. Presenting a self-evident fact—even in a fancy multicolor chart—is not persuading me of anything."

"I don't get it," said Emily.

"Everything costs more than it used to!" Mr. Henderson's voice grew louder than seemed strictly necessary. "That fact alone does not constitute a reason for those things to suddenly be made free."

He stood and went to the board and wrote a bunch of words. "Sets. Costumes. Lights. Don't these cost money?"

"I guess." Emily felt the prospect of extra credit slipping through her fingers.

Mr. Henderson wrote some more. "Actors. Musicians. Ushers. Stagehands. Do you think all these people should work *for nothing?*"

"Nope," Emily conceded.

He wrote again, really big this time. "Directors. Choreographers. Composers, book writers, lyricists! Are you suggesting that all these creative people should labor for years and years to create Broadway musicals for Emily Pearl's personal amusement without ever getting paid a dime?"

"Okay, I get it," Emily said, shrinking back. Mr. Henderson looked ready to burst a vein. He must have seen the fear on her face.

"Emily, Emily, Emily," he said. "I'm being hard on you, and there is a reason. I too am a fan of the theatre. There was a time when I dreamed of writing for Broadway myself. Believe it or not, some of us started out with bigger dreams than teaching high school English and directing the spring musical." He looked around the classroom sadly. "Not that this job is going to save me. I can hardly afford to see a Broadway show myself more than once in a blue moon. But at least I get benefits. Health insurance, pension . . ." Emily found it hard to follow his train of thought, and her mind wandered. "You know we're doing *Fiddler* this year, auditions are next week . . . ya-hah-deedle-deedle-bubba-bubba-deedle-deedle-dum . . ."

In another minute she was going to be late for Spanish. "Sorry, Mr. Henderson," Emily said, trying her best not to sound snotty, "but what is your point, exactly?"

He handed her essay back to her. "My point is that this is a wish, not an argument. How *could* Broadway shows be free? *You* figure it out! *Persuade* me it'll work! Convince me it's both possible *and* a good idea!"

"Okay," Emily said, feeling tiny.

"By Monday! And no *Aurora*!" he yelled after her as she slunk out of the classroom.

8

"JELLICLE SONGS FOR JELLICLE CATS"

Cats

**1982. Music by Andrew Lloyd Webber, lyrics based
on *Old Possum's Book of Practical Cats* by T. S. Eliot,
additional lyrics by Trevor Nunn and Richard Stilgoe**

By the following Saturday they were no closer to figuring out
Ian's maddening clue, but it was a special Saturday nevertheless. It was Philip's sixteenth birthday, and Emily was the only
person who remembered.

This was not entirely true, but Philip wished it were. Early
that morning the fax machine in Philip's mother's bedroom
had spit out a page from Wilmington, but it was too garbled to
read more than "H py B th ay lv Mo." For some reason Philip
found this depressing.

Mark, cheaply, had made Philip a fake ID and left it on his
pillow. Philip stashed it in his sock drawer; he didn't want it
but at least it wasn't some awful mocking present, like a Village People CD. And not Philip's father but the second Mrs.
Nebbling had sent a card from Seattle, where they now lived.

"Best wishes from me and Dad," she'd written. Mr. Nebbling had not signed his own name. The ten-dollar bill inside the card wasn't even the crisp new kind people usually give, but a thin and tattered one that had lived inside many different wallets since leaving the mint.

"Intermission M&M's are on me today," Philip said to Emily as he smoothed the bill flat against his thigh. They were on the train, heading westbound into the city. "Or maybe I should use it to buy a car. Tough choice."

"Your dad married a jerk," Emily said, staring out the window at the familiar landscape of small, weathered houses and abandoned automobile tires. There were plenty of really swank houses on Long Island, but not along the train tracks.

Emily wanted to say something else, to comfort or at least distract Philip from this abomination of a birthday card and the fact that his father was the real jerk for moving across the country and starting a garlic farm with his new hippy-dippy wife, thus rendering him unable to pay more than a token amount in child support. (The first and last time Philip had gone to Seattle for a visit he'd had an anxiety attack at the top of the Space Needle, and now he was skittish about heights. The smell of garlic had also become a problem.)

"So, Philip," she said, with her most winning smile, "what do you think we should do when we get to the city?"

Philip shifted in his seat. "I dunno. How about we wait on line for rush tickets to *Aurora*?" He was trying to sound playful, but it fell flat. "You know, try something new!"

Emily reached into her *Aurora* messenger bag. "Well, we *could* do that," she said, "but then what would we do with these?" She took a slim, rectangular envelope out of her bag and handed it to Philip, who was genuinely astonished.

Inside were two full-price *Aurora* tickets, one hundred dollars each. Eighth-row center orchestra, the best seats in the house. A special birthday treat, purchased months in advance by Emily with a painstakingly accumulated nest egg of baby-sitting money and a little boost from Grandma Rose. She really was very good at keeping secrets.

"Emileeeeeeeeeee," he cried, hugging her hard. "You are the best, best, best, best!"

"I know," she said, very pleased. "I am."

It was a delicious kind of fun for Emily and Philip to saunter past all the regulars on the rush ticket line, after a long lazy browse through the cast album section at the Virgin Megastore in Times Square.

"You guys are so late!" called Ruthie, from the line. "You'll never get a ticket now!" Ruthie was in her fifties and worked as a paralegal during the week, but on Saturday mornings she put on a push-up bustier, red satin hot pants, and a crazy-quilt poncho with matching floppy hat and waited for *Aurora* tickets with her boyfriend, Morris, who was nowhere to be seen at the moment.

Philip merely grinned, but Emily couldn't resist waving the pair of hundred-dollar orchestra seat tickets in front of Ruthie's nose.

"Smell you!" Ruthie squealed. "You musta got a good report card or something."

"It's a special occasion," Emily said. "It's Philip's birth—"

"Hey!" It was Morris, heading toward them with the limping, rolling, bowlegged walk of a peg-legged pirate. He carried two cups of coffee in the Edison's signature take-out cardboard cups, which bore the dual masks of comedy and tragedy, each savoring a cup of joe. Comedy seemed to like the coffee; tragedy, not so much.

Morris did not dress in *Aurora* costume, thank goodness. He was a grizzled phone company retiree, a cantankerous theatre freak who'd seen every show since *Porgy and Bess* and held violently strong opinions about all of them.

"Damn, Ruthie," he called as he approached. "This toe is killing me. I hope whatever show it is posts a notice soon—" But when he saw Emily and Philip, he stopped.

"Hey, Morris," said Philip. "Seen anything good lately?" It was a joke, since they all knew Morris went to the theatre constantly and hated everything, which apparently only fueled his desire to see more. (Emily had once questioned the logic of this, and Morris explained that bad shows demonstrated the Pringles Effect: they tasted kind of gross, but in a way that made you want to keep eating.)

"Don't mess with me," Morris growled. "I'm in pain."

"It's the Toe," Ruthie explained in a hushed voice. "The Closing Toe."

Emily and Philip looked confused.

"Whenever a show's about to close, the Toe swells up and hurts like the devil," Morris said. "It came on me all of a sudden, 'bout eight o'clock this morning."

"The longer the show's been running, the more it hurts," Ruthie added. "When they announced *Cats* was finally closing, my baby could hardly walk for a week."

"Thorn in your paw, huh?" The Closing Toe concept was so beyond even the normal insanity of Broadway that Philip couldn't resist being fresh. Teasing Morris required delicacy, though, because his temper was easy to provoke. One time he and another guy on the rush line got into a shoving match over whether or not Bernadette Peters was miscast in the revival of *Annie Get Your Gun,* and they wouldn't stop even after the police were called.

"Go ahead and mock," growled Morris. "The Toe has never been wrong."

"Thorn in your paw, that's pretty funny," Emily whispered to Philip.

"It's a jellicle joke," Philip whispered back. "For jellicle cats." Emily had to bite her lip not to crack up.

"Thanks for the java, baby," Ruthie said, taking her coffee and dropping a kiss on Morris's nose. "So what'd you think of that play last night at Soho Rep?"

"Preposterous," Morris declared. "The dramatic structure was all over the map. Avant-garde? Avant-crap, more like it . . ."

Morris's diatribe filled Emily's mind with a thought that seemed so incontrovertibly right she couldn't believe it hadn't occurred to her before. Who were the crankiest theatre cranks she knew? SAVEMEFROMAURORA and Morris, of course! Could they be one and the same?

"You!" she said, unable to control herself. "You should be ashamed of yourself, hassling kids on the Internet!"

"Keep it down!" said Morris, looking around in a panic. "Watch what you say, little girl! The cops are everywhere. Now what the hell are you talking about?"

"You know what I mean," said Emily, in a quieter but still insistent voice. "You know *exactly* what I mean. SAVEME."

"SAVEME? You mean that loudmouthed misanthrope who hangs around the Broadway chat rooms, spewing bile and vitriol?" Morris looked genuinely hurt. "And you think that's me?"

"My Morris is an idealist," said Ruthie. "A man of high standards! That's why I *wuv* him." Morris blushed, and Ruthie started crooning in his ear: "Never be enough! My love for you will never be enough!"

Emily didn't know whether to apologize or keep pressing, but she didn't get the chance to do either because a box office staff member started yelling instructions at the rush line, as if everyone didn't already know the drill. "Hey," said Morris. "How come you guys aren't on the line? You lose your spot?"

"We already have tickets," said Philip.

"Eighth-row orchestra," said Emily proudly. "It's Philip's birthday. He's sixteen today."

Ruthie gave Philip a hug, but Morris turned away, wincing. He gingerly put a little weight on his foot. "Getting worse," he muttered. "Feels like a three-year run, at least."

Silly Broadway, thought Emily fondly, with its Pringles Effect, prophetic toes, and strange, superstitious rituals. Ian had long ago explained to Emily and Philip how you were never supposed to say "good luck" to an actor (it was bad luck; instead you said "break a leg" or "merde"). Even worse was to mention Shakespeare's *Mac*—well, the Scottish Play, as it was always called, because to say the play's name was to invoke a mysterious curse that often caused scenery to collapse upon actors, theatres to burn down, or other, often fatal mishaps to befall the production.

Emily's favorite Broadway tradition was the Gypsy Robe. She'd never seen it, but her understanding was that it was basically a decorated bathrobe, presented by the chorus of one show to that of another show before curtain on opening night. Each show added its own memento to the robe—a flower from the leading lady's hat, or an autographed patch of fabric from a costume—and awarded it to the gypsy with the most Broadway credits.

Sometimes Emily imagined herself receiving the robe and being crowned Queen of the Gypsies, traipsing from dressing room to dressing room and wishing everyone *merde, merde, merde*. It would be a royal feeling indeed.

For now, though, it was special enough to be downstairs in the orchestra section, instead of up in the balcony where they usually sat. Emily knew the Rialto Theatre like the back of her hand, but she let the usher direct her to her seat. It made her feel like a princess.

"Thank you," she said to the usher, distinctly, like Audrey Hepburn, as she was handed her *Playbill*. "Thank you *so* much."

There was much to look at, in those sacred moments before an *Aurora* performance began. The Rialto was an ornate relic from a bygone age, meticulously restored, its cavernous ceiling bedecked with cherubs and angels, gilded harps and carved medallions. What mad genius could imagine such a place? Sometimes Emily and Philip would just sit there gazing upward, wordlessly nudging each other and pointing at some freshly noticed detail.

"Cell phone?" Philip asked.

"Got it," said Emily. "Happy birthday, Philip."

"Emily," he said, full of feeling. "Thank you so much."

The lights started to dim, and Emily wondered if she might give Philip an impulsive birthday kiss. If Stephanie could do it, why couldn't she? But before she could decide, the houselights faded to black. A moment later the overture began; as for the kiss—she'd forgotten almost completely about it.

9

"SIXTEEN GOING ON SEVENTEEN"

The Sound of Music

1959. Music by Richard Rodgers,
lyrics by Oscar Hammerstein II,
book by Howard Lindsay and Russel Crouse

Maybe it was the awesome seats or a whiff of birthday magic, but that performance of *Aurora* was inarguably the best they'd ever seen. The audience was transported: laughing uproariously at the funny parts, gasping with surprise at the plot twists, and melting into tears at the point in the story where Aurora, despite the disapproval of her friends and family and the increasing difficulties posed by her own mysterious illness, sacrifices everything for one last chance at happiness with Enrique, the endearing yet chronically unreliable love of her life.

Enrique was no longer being played by the original performer, but by a big-name teen heartthrob more famous for being the lead singer in a boy band than for any kind of serious acting. Today it didn't matter who played the part, though, because Marlena Ortiz was on fire. She *was* Aurora, and Aurora was her, and the boy-band star sobbed real tears onstage as Marlena looked tenderly into his eyes and sang:

> *"Never be enough,*
> *Ten thousand nights would never be enough . . ."*

Emily and Philip hugged each other for a long time after the curtain call was done (it seemed to last forever; no one wanted to stop clapping). They hugged and hugged and none of the people waiting to get out of their row minded, because everyone was feeling the same way.

Getting autographs at the stage door had become part of their *Aurora* ritual since the first preview. By now Emily and Philip knew the doorman by name, and the cast members slapped them high fives as they dashed out to their postshow lives.

"Philip! Emily! Darrrrrlings!"

Stephanie exploded from the stage door and sang out their names like a melody. She gave Philip an extraspecial smile.

"The show was unbelievable today, Stephanie," Emily burbled. Even though she knew Stephanie was an ordinary, flawed, and somewhat potty-mouthed human being in real life, there was something so thrilling about watching her emerge from the theatre after a show. It made Emily feel hyper, nervous, badly dressed—starstruck, though she hated to admit it. "The audience went nuts."

"I know," Stephanie said, in a confidential tone. "There was a rumor backstage that some Hollywood people were here to see Marlena. She sure turned on the juice, didn't she?"

Philip held his pen and *Playbill* out to Stephanie. She laughed and said, "I feel kinda stupid giving you my autograph, since we're such good friends now." Stephanie waggled her eyebrows suggestively. "Special friends, right, Phil?"

Nobody called Philip "Phil" except his mother and Mark, but when Stephanie said the name it was a whole different thing. Philip blushed and grinned. "It's his birthday!" Emily explained, elbowing him in the ribs. "We want the whole cast to sign the *Playbill* with today's date on it."

"I've got everybody but you and Marlena," said Philip.

"I know," giggled Stephanie. "We're always the slow-pokes." She signed her name really big, right on the cover of his *Playbill*. "Whoops! Guess I didn't leave much room for Marlena. Birthday, huh?" She handed him back his Sharpie. "That explains why you're looking so very handsome and grown-up today."

Stephanie stepped close to Philip, who only now realized what was coming his way and was instantly grateful for the breath mint he'd been sucking on during the second act.

"Happy birthday, baby," Stephanie said. She stretched up on tippy-toe and kissed Philip three times: once on each cheek, and once more, very gently—here Emily got embarrassed and had to look away—on the lips. "I wish I could party with you guys but I have a dinner date before the second show—you know how it is!"

Philip felt like he might be having an out-of-body experience, which was a shame, since this was the most fun his body had had in a while. "Thank you," he managed to croak. He didn't dare look at Emily.

"Good night!" Stephanie kept waving to them as she trotted to the curb in her fur-trimmed, high-heeled boots. A taxi was waiting for her. "Make sure he has a good time!" she yelled to Emily.

"I will," Emily tried to call back, but it didn't come out loudly enough for anyone to hear. She had a weird feeling in the pit of her stomach. Behind her, Marlena Ortiz had just stepped out the stage door. Everyone was screaming and Philip had already turned his attention to getting the star's autograph on his *Playbill*.

If he wants a birthday kiss from Marlena, he can ask for it himself, Emily thought, in an uncharacteristically snappish way. Usually she would push to the front of the crowd to say hi to Marlena, but this time she stayed where she was.

As she stood there, glowering with a kind of irritation she couldn't quite name, she saw Morris limping with determination toward Eighth Avenue, like an escaped convict with a ball and chain still shackled to his leg.

"Wait!" Emily yelled, dashing into the street. She was nothing if not impulsive. "Morris, wait up!" Fearlessly dodging traffic, Emily zigzagged between the honking cars until she caught up with him.

"I just wanted to apologize for thinking you were SAVEME," Emily said, blocking his path and placing her hand on his arm.

Morris waved her away with his gnarled, nicotine-stained fingers. "I don't lose sleep about what other people think," he said. "I have my own thoughts to occupy me."

"I guess it was dumb." Emily sighed. "I just really wish I knew who he was. He bugs me."

"Get a life, honey," Morris said, not unkindly. "Then you'll forget all about it. Now I gotta go, Ruthie's working the night shift at her law firm and I'm on my way to Don't Tell Mama—the pianist starts at five."

"I was wondering," Emily said before he could bolt, "if you could give me some advice about this paper I have to write? For school?" Mr. Henderson had given her until Monday for her revised persuasive essay; she still had no clue what to put in it, but one good rant from Morris and she'd have enough material to argue her case before the Supreme Court. "I had this idea that tickets to Broadway shows should be free, you know? But my teacher asked me to figure out how that might work, so I thought I would ask someone with a lot of experience, and I realized you were probably the most knowledgeable person there is when it comes to Broadway."

"If you think flattery is gonna get me to do your homework for you," growled Morris, "you are barking up the wrong—"

"Emileeeeeeeeeee!" It was Ian's familiar tenor, carrying Mermanesquely above the din of Forty-fourth Street. He ran over to them, breathless and upset. "Oh. My. God. I have to tell you something. I think it's bad but I'm not sure."

"Whatever you heard—ouch!—why not keep it to yourself, kid?" Morris winced and rubbed his foot.

Ian ignored Morris and spoke urgently to Emily. "I got this e-mail, from my 'friend.' The one *sur la plage*. The one who *knows* things."

"The Actors' Chapel is on West Forty-eighth!" thundered Morris as he hopped on one foot in agony. "Tell your secrets to the Great Casting Director Upstairs!"

"I don't know what it means," said Ian, clutching Emily by the shoulders. "It's something about *Aurora* and a stop clause—"

"Hey, Em, wait up!" Philip was yelling as he loped across

64

the street waving his *Playbill*. "Marlena wrote that I'm her 'Number One Fan,' look—"

Philip saw Ian and Morris and stopped short. "Hey," he said. "What's up?"

Everyone was silent.

"Did you say 'stop clause'?" asked Morris, now very still.

"Yes!" cried Ian. "That doesn't sound very positive, does it? A go clause, that would be positive. But a stop clause—"

"Shhhhhhh!" Morris yanked himself free of Emily, wheeled around in place, and pounded his fist into his hand. "Listen!" he shouted, before he realized he was shouting. "Come here, children, come here." The streets were getting packed with people as all the Broadway shows started to let out. Emily, Philip, and Ian had to stand very close to Morris to hear him.

"Where did you hear this nefarious news?" said Morris.

"From—a friend," Ian said.

"And you believe your friend is telling the truth?" Morris asked sternly. "Not just flinging the crap around, like everybody else in this town?"

"I do," said Ian, his voice shaking. "I just don't know what it means."

Morris glanced left and right, checking for spies. "The stop clause." His voice sank to a whisper. "The dreaded stop clause."

Emily opened her mouth to ask a question, but Morris held up his hand.

"I had a feeling," he moaned. "This damn toe! I almost said something before, but I didn't want to spoil the show for you, not once I found out it's the kid's birthday."

Philip, whose head was still in the clouds from Marlena's

autograph and Stephanie's kiss, had no clue what was going on. He laughed. "Didn't you see the matinee today? It was amazing. Nothing could spoil *Aurora* for us, Morris, don't be silly."

Ian squeaked, like a mouse under a cat's paw. Morris looked first at Ian, then at Philip, then at Emily.

"You guys don't know what the stop clause is?"

The three of them shook their heads.

"It means," Morris said, "the show's closing."

10

"DON'T TELL MAMA"

Cabaret
1966. Music by John Kander, lyrics by Fred Ebb, book by Joe Masteroff

As Morris led them around the corner to Don't Tell Mama, the only thought in Philip's mind was this: how had he not seen this coming?

What was the point of his spreadsheets, his meticulous crunching of the box office figures, his *Variety* subscription and his performance logs and all the rest of it, if something as momentous and life-altering and beyond all everyday concerns as a Broadway musical—a Tony Award winner, mind you!—could be obliterated by something called *the dreaded stop clause*?

Surely there had been some warning embedded in his spreadsheets, some sign of impending disaster that he'd missed, like an idiot. *I made a mistake,* he thought, his fingers trembling. *A stupid, obvious mistake, and now it's all going to come crashing down—*

"Morris, darling! Table for—four?" The plump waitress was wearing twin streaks of teal blue eyeshadow above her enormous false eyelashes, which she batted shamelessly at Morris. Then she looked at Emily. "You need a tissue, honey?"

Emily nodded. She hadn't even known she was crying, but when she touched her face, her cheeks were wet.

The waitress grabbed some paper napkins from the bar as she led the four of them to a booth near the piano. She handed the wad of napkins to Emily and bent over to stage-whisper loudly in her ear. "Whoever got the part, honey, she's not half as good as you. Don't ask me how I can tell—I have a nose for talent." The waitress inhaled deeply, as if demonstrating her nose's special ability, and left.

Emily, Ian, and Philip sat down without taking off their coats. Ian was making a pathetic whimpering noise every thirty seconds or so.

"All right. We're here. Now please, Morris, tell us: what exactly is 'the dreaded stop clause'?" Philip was trying not to sound hysterical. Morris had flatly refused to discuss the matter any further on the street, which he claimed was "full of ears." It had taken three excruciating minutes to make it around the corner to Don't Tell Mama, the famed piano bar on West Forty-sixth, and Philip's head was gathering enough steam to start whistling out both his ears.

Morris looked around the room. The accompanist had just arrived and was still chatting with the bartender, a safe distance away from their table. "I'll try to make this quick." He sighed. "But nothing is simple in show business."

One Tanqueray martini (dry, with an olive) and three Shirley Temples later (they'd asked for tap water, but the waitress brought these over on the house, since Morris was a regular), Ian, Emily, and Philip were still struggling to understand Morris's explanation.

"So, the producers of the show rent the theatre from the theatre owner?" said Philip. "And the 'stop clause' says if ticket sales fall below a certain number for two weeks in a row, the theatre owner can cancel the lease and throw the show out?"

"Zactly," said Morris, glancing about. "Keep your voice down."

"And *Aurora*'s ticket sales fell below that number?" asked Emily, dumbfounded.

"Must have, if this stop clause business is true." Morris glared at Ian, who was staring morosely at the maraschino cherry in his silly pink cocktail.

If only we'd bought more tickets! Emily thought, her heart filling with remorse. *It might have made all the difference!*

"I saw that dip in the box office!" cried Philip, remembering his spreadsheets. "But the weather was horrible that week. Ticket sales for all the shows went down."

"Don't matter why, kid." Morris chomped on the olive. "Stevie Stephenson—he's the fella that owns the Rialto—he's not a sentimental guy. And he's the lead producer on *Aurora* to begin with. Who's he gonna argue with, himself?"

"But from a business standpoint," insisted Philip, who was determined to comprehend this, "you have a show that's selling, on average, eighty-three percent, and you're going to close it on the chance that the next show will do better?"

"Correct," Morris said. The accompanist had finally settled

at the piano and was now playing rapid scales up and down the keys to warm up.

"It's not fair!" Emily wailed. "*Aurora* is so much better than any other show they could bring in!"

Morris made a frantic shushing gesture at Emily, which just made her start crying again. Already the two chorus boys at the next table had taken out their cell phones and were making urgent, whispered calls, all while glancing at Morris's table.

"But what if the new show's a flop?" Ian asked. "I mean, it might be. Nobody knows what's going to be a hit!"

"It's a gamble. So what? So's the stock market!" Morris was turning red with exasperation. "So's a horse race. You want a sure thing, put your money under the mattress!"

"There's only One Sure Thing in show business, honey, and I don't mean talent!" the waitress interjected as she slapped their check down on the table. "Take me, for instance! In my day"—none of them were sure which day she meant, but it probably wasn't recent—"I was gonna be the next Chita Rivera! Looks, voice, *legs*. I had it all." She rolled her eyes upward, toward the balcony of her mind. "But the right part never came along."

The waitress's voice grew deep and round and fake British sounding. "The chorus is *not* for me. Some people were meant to be *stars*." Her grand exit was only slightly marred by some people at a nearby table demanding water refills as she passed.

Philip, Emily, and Ian watched her walk away. "She was something, all right," Morris remarked. "An ugly voice, but you could hear it all the way to the back of the theatre. Now let me ask *you* something, dancing boy!" His eyes pinned Ian to the back of his chair. "Who the hell told you this 'news'? Don't give me that 'I promised not to tell' crap! You told, you ruined the kid's birthday, now own it like a man."

"His name," whimpered Ian, "is Lester."

"Lester!" Morris pounded the table. "From Florida?"

"Palm Beach," Ian nodded, turning pale.

"Wait!" said Philip. "What are the odds you both know a guy named Lester in Florida and it's the same guy?"

"Odds? It's practically a sure thing." Morris scratched fiercely at the back of his neck. "This is the theatre, kiddo. It's ten people. You've heard of those small towns in flyover country where everybody knows each other's business? Talented dreamers run away from those towns and come to New York to breathe the air of freedom. Then they get into a Broadway show and guess what? Aunt Betty's in your underwear drawer all over again."

What? thought Emily. She'd zoned out for one minute and now they were talking about underwear? It wasn't that she'd lost interest; she'd just suddenly realized that she and Philip had missed their usual train back to Long Island. The next one wasn't for an hour. She'd be getting home exceptionally late, and her parents thought she and Philip were at another PSAT prep class. What cover story would she cook up this time?

"Lester!" Morris went on. "No, no, no, *no*, Nanette!" He smacked Ian on the head. "You ruined the kid's birthday for nothing."

"Ahhh!" Emily keened, expressing neither joy nor despair, but rather the sensation of her last nerve finally snapping. "You mean it's not *true*? The show's *not* closing?"

"If it came from Lester, it's crap." Morris snorted. "He's a crap flinger. Professional! An on-the-payroll crap flinger."

Ian's mouth fell open. "You know Lester?"

"Everybody knows Lester!" Morris drained his glass. "Stevie Stephenson, the guy who owns the Rialto? Lester's his nephew. What a nimrod. He keeps a little place in Florida so

71

the whole family can claim it as a primary residence and not pay any income tax. That's his job, to live in Florida and fling crap. Sweet gig, huh? He told you some happy horse poo about who wrote *Aurora*, too, am I right?"

Ian slumped down in his seat. "Uh, yeah," he admitted. "Did I fall for something?"

"Did you ever! That's Lester's other job—every couple of months he starts a new rumor about who wrote *Aurora*. For a while he had people saying it was Jerry Herman. Then Sondheim. Then the headwaiter at Sardi's. What a joker."

"But why would he lie?" said Philip, still struggling to understand. "What's the point?"

"Sometimes it's to impress some cute young chorus boy," Morris intoned ominously. "Otherwise it's just red herrings. Keeps the public confused. So far it's worked. Who did he tell you it was?"

Ian was beginning to hyperventilate. "Oprah Winfrey," he said, barely audible.

"Oprah Winfrey!" Morris guffawed. "That's rich. Jeez, I can't wait to tell that one to Ruthie."

Emily looked at Morris with new respect. He was old and wise as the hills. Old Man Broadway, that was Morris.

"Morris," she said suddenly. "Do *you* know who wrote *Aurora*?"

Morris shook his head. "Believe me, if it could be known, I'd know it by now." Without asking, he grabbed the maraschino cherry out of Philip's drink and popped it in his mouth. "Nobody knows who wrote *Aurora*, and nobody will ever know. Don't waste your time thinking about it."

Philip didn't care about the cherry, but his head was starting to throb from trying to make sense of all this new data. "So—the show's *not* going to close, then?"

Morris shrugged. "All shows close sooner or later," he said. "Even *Cats* closed. You can't take it personally."

"But what about your toe?" asked Emily.

Morris hesitated, then shrugged again. "Who knows? Maybe it's gonna rain."

"It violates all concepts of rational self-interest!" Philip ranted. "It defies standard economic theory! Unless you could predict with a very high degree of certainty that the new show would do substantially better than the one you were kicking out . . ."

Philip, whose birthday it still was, continued in this agitated vein as the three of them headed crosstown on West Forty-sixth Street. It was only a little after six, but night had fallen and the theatre district was lit up like a thousand blinking Christmas trees.

"Relax, Philip. It's not true, okay?" The false alarm about *Aurora* closing had been debunked, and Emily was only too eager to forget about it. She poked Ian. "Say something," she mouthed.

"I'm really sorry, Philip." Ian sounded convincingly humble. "I can't believe I did this to you, especially on your birthday. That'll teach me to repeat stupid rumors."

"Forget it, please," Philip said. "You didn't ruin my birthday, okay? Honest. I had a great time today." He smiled at Emily. "Orchestra seats! And a great show. And some, uh, excitement, too."

"I'll walk you to Penn Station, okay? It'll be my 'Penn-ance.'" Ian lived with his parents on the Upper West Side, but he didn't often mention that fact, since it made him seem more like the high school student he really was and less like a star in the making. "But you have to entertain me along the way. Show question: which humungous star auditioned for but did *not* get the part of Mary Magdalene in the original Broadway company of *Jesus Christ Superstar?*"

"Easy," snorted Philip. "Bette Midler, everyone knows that."

"Consider it a freebie," said Ian, warming to the game. "Name the Broadway show that 'The Man I Love' was written for."

"Trick question! It's *Lady Be Good*, but 'The Man I Love' was cut before the show opened," said Philip, without hesitation. "1924. Music by George Gershwin, lyrics by Ira Gershwin, book by Guy Bolton and Fred Thompson." He grinned. "The song was later added to *Strike up the Band*, which closed out of town, and *Rosalie*, where it was cut once again."

Everything is fine now. Emily willed herself to believe it. *Everything is fine.*

11

"SOON IT'S GONNA RAIN"

The Fantasticks
1960 (Off-Broadway). Music by Harvey Schmidt,
lyrics and book by Tom Jones

Sunday it rained all day.

That explains Morris's toe, Emily thought with relief. She looked out her bedroom window and saw the gray sky, the trees in the front yard swaying in a blustery wind, the surface of the street dark with rain. Most people would have called it bad weather, but to Emily it was meteorological proof that everything was right with *Aurora*, and thus, the world.

Further proof: her parents had gone to the movies last night and had not even been home to witness or inquire about her late arrival time. Surely this was another incontrovertible sign that Emily's world was right as—well, as rain.

And yet she felt uneasy. Yesterday's stop clause scare was the kind of close call that left you looking both ways before crossing one-way streets. What was it Morris had said?

All shows close sooner or later.

Even Cats *closed.*

Huh.

Buried somewhere in that self-evident truth was a warning that eventually, inevitably, Emily would have to plan for a life after—a life beyond—a life without—

But not yet. She let the curtains close and climbed back into bed. She still had that stupid essay to write, but another half hour of sleep couldn't hurt. It was Sunday, after all.

Why Broadway Shows Should Be Free
A Persuasive Essay by Emily Pearl
Second Draft

Broadway shows are wonderful, but to pay a hundred dollars for a ticket is too much. What if a person has to buy food? Or pay rent? Or is perhaps too young to have a job? Even so, such people might love to see a Broadway musical, and don't they have the right? I think Broadway shows should be free for all. Here's how it could be accomplished.

First, the producers should stop charging money for tickets.

Second,

Third—

And in conclusion, that is how Broadway shows could be free.

Those pesky middle paragraphs. The problem was *how*. A few hours' research had only confirmed Mr. Henderson's objections. Not only were millions of dollars required to get a show to opening night, but keeping it running cost a staggering sum every week.

For some reason Emily couldn't fathom, this number was called the "nut." The nut included the cost of renting the theatre, salaries for the actors, musicians and stagehands, the weekly advertising budget, the royalties that were paid to the creative team—the list went on and on. (Emily suddenly wondered how much it cost to replenish the fake flower petals for *Aurora's* curtain call. The tiny circles of pink and red tissue paper had rained down on her scores of times, but it hadn't previously occurred to her that they cost money.)

As if this weren't discouraging enough, Emily also discovered that Broadway theatres had something called a *capacity*. That was a fancy way of saying the theatre only had so many seats (the Rialto had 1,545, to be exact). A Broadway musical played eight shows a week; union rules forbade adding any more.

Emily even wrote it out mathematically (Philip would have been so impressed):

> *(# of seats)* × *(8 performances a week)* × *(ticket price)* = *maximum amount of money any show could make per week*

The number of seats couldn't go up, the number of performances couldn't go up—Emily was no math whiz, but even she could see that the only thing that *could* go up was the ticket price.

Emily ripped the notes for her paper out of her notepad and crushed them into a crinkly yellow ball. If, by giving this assignment, Mr. Henderson had wanted to demonstrate that facts had the power to persuade, he'd done it. Emily was persuaded: there was no way Broadway shows could be free. As far as she could tell, it was nearly impossible for them to be produced at all.

Philip also awoke on Sunday with an uneasy feeling. Even in the abstract, the stop clause concept was causing him no end of discomfort. He didn't like the idea behind it: everything could seem fine, life was putt-putting along without any significant bumps in the road, and then—one moment of weakness or inattention or plain bad luck and goodbye, Charlie, as Emily's Grandma Rose liked to say.

He took out his *Aurora* spreadsheets and tried to calm himself with numbers. But his mind kept racing back in time to that awful day three years before when he'd sat at this very table, listening to his mother's end of a phone conversation that contained the following information: his father was getting remarried only six months after moving out—the minute the divorce was final, basically—and he and his new garlic-farming wife would be relocating to the other side of the continent of North America immediately following the wedding. . . .

After the phone call Mrs. Nebbling locked herself in her bedroom, and Mark yelled a few choice swear words he'd learned from Grand Theft Auto. Then he stormed out to spend the night at a friend's house.

Alone, ignored, abandoned, thirteen-year-old Philip couldn't hold still—he paced around the living room, which was still piled high with unpacked boxes (they had just moved into Birchwood Gardens, and they were all trying not to mention how much smaller it was than their old house). He shoved his hands into his pockets and took them out again. He literally felt like he might explode.

So he swiped the grocery money from the glass jar on the kitchen counter, walked at top speed with his head down the whole way to the train station, and headed into the city on his own, which he'd started doing since his father left. Rules and limits didn't seem to apply anymore.

He bought his ticket on the train, which cost extra, but he didn't care. He half ran from Penn Station to Times Square, and then, as the razor edge of his mood finally began to soften, he walked up to the first box office window he saw and bought what turned out to be the very last available ticket to the very first public performance of a new musical called *Aurora*. . . .

"Dude!" Mark slapped a greasy pizza box right on top of Philip's papers. "I made you some lunch. Bon appétit!"

"Gross," Philip said, snatching his spreadsheets away before they were ruined. "I'm not hungry."

"Watching your figure for the ladies, huh? Have you kissed that Emily yet?" Mark made noisy kissy lips.

"Would you please just die?" Philip retorted. "Emily and I are just friends, I keep telling you that. Do you kiss your friends?"

" 'Just friends!' I rest my case, Your Honor. The 'just friends' alibi is Exhibit Gay, *Philip Nebbling versus the State of Denial*." Mark grabbed a hot slice out of the box and took a big, cheesy bite. The stink of garlic hit Philip like a slap. " 'Just friends,' " Mark said, the sauce dripping down his chin. "That's a good one."

Thankfully, this unpleasant conversation was interrupted by the little snippet of "Never Be Enough" Philip had made into his IM alarm:

Never be enough,
My love for you could
Never be enough . . .

It was Emily, summoning him to the computer for three o'clock, Sunday matinee time. He and Emily would chat on-line and play the overture together and Philip would feel much better.

Philip moved a pile of dirty laundry from the chair to the floor and sat down in front of the screen.

AURORAROX: hey
AURORAROX: u there?
AURORAROX: u have to be there u have to be there, pleeeeeeeze
BwayPhil: Okay! Relax, I'm here.
AURORAROX: OMG! have you seen the message boards?
BwayPhil: No, what's going on?
AURORAROX: OMG OMG you have to look
BwayPhil: Which one?
AURORAROX: all of them
AURORAROX: just look
AURORAROX: i'll wait

With a few clicks Philip got the TheatreGeeks.com message boards open on his screen.

Something's closing, did you hear?
I heard something long-running
I heard it might be a stop clause situation—
That stinks, producers are such greedy bullies
Yeah but there wouldn't be any shows without them . . .

He switched to a different message board.

I think it's phantom
probably, that's been running 4ever
still sells out though, who'd kick out phantom?
Well it's not "lion king"
No, you still can't get tickets to lion king—

That was BroadwayDish.com. There were dozens of these sites; Philip had all the big ones bookmarked.

Where'd you hear?
I read it on ThespNet.com
I read it on BackstageGossip.com
I heard it from a friend in the business—she's in the chorus of Mamma Mia, she heard it from her friend who's the assistant stage manager at Avenue Q who got it from his friend who's the swing for Hairspray—
What did he say?!!!
Only that it's a show no one would expect, the theatre owner is closing on a technicality to make room for something else
Something even bigger
but no one knows what

Philip's heart was beating very fast. His ears suddenly filled with a horrible, piercing, high-pitched sound.

AURORAROX: p, you there?
AURORAROX: ?
BwayPhil: Sorry, back now!
BwayPhil: Mark burned PopTarts & the smoke alarms went off.

BwayPhil: I had to go yank out all the batteries to shut them up.

AURORAROX: oh

AURORAROX: so did you see

BwayPhil: I did.

AURORAROX: it makes me so nervous

AURORAROX: what if it's true after all

AURORAROX: what lester said about aurora

AURORAROX: and the stupid stupid stop clause—

BwayPhil: Hang on now—

BwayPhil: Has it occurred to you that maybe WE started this rumor?

AURORAROX: ?

BwayPhil: Remember? There were those guys in Don't Tell Mama.

BwayPhil: Maybe they heard us talking.

BwayPhil: Or maybe somebody saw Morris limping.

BwayPhil: Or maybe it's just a coincidence.

BwayPhil: Okay?

AURORAROX: okay

AURORAROX: maybe . . .

12

"A BOOK REPORT ON PETER RABBIT"

You're a Good Man, Charlie Brown
1967 (Off-Broadway), 1971 (Broadway).
Music, lyrics, and book by Clark Gesner

Monday was a dark day.

In the theatre a "dark day" meant it was the actors' day off, there was no performance, the theatre was "dark."

In real life, of course, a dark day was one that was full of dread and despair. It was the day on which you would be required to turn in a long-overdue paper you have not, for the most part, written. A day when there was nothing but cold pizza for breakfast, since your brother's definition of the five food groups was pizza, Fritos, salsa, more pizza, and Red Bull.

Above all, a dark day was one in which the thing that gave your life meaning and purpose, the ritual that filled your Saturday afternoons with music and your tender heart with joy, might or might not be threatened with oblivion, and there was no way to find out for sure.

Monday was a dark day indeed.

Even Marlena Ortiz was having a bad day. . . .

"Thank you for all your concern!" Marlena Ortiz typed. The blog format made it look like the thumbnail-sized head shot of her on the screen was talking, and the picture seemed so happy and carefree that she was often tempted to write really nasty things coming out of its mouth. She didn't, of course. Marlena had worked awfully hard to get this far; she wasn't about to screw it up.

Marlena typically spent twenty minutes a day posting on the official *Aurora* blog. She answered questions from fans and slipped them thrilling tidbits of personal info ("Hey, I'm from the Bronx too!"). When she was pressed for time, she'd make sure to post a "hello" message so "her people" knew she'd at least logged on to read their gushing. Her contract didn't require it, but the Aurorafans loved it. *Aurora* had been good to Marlena and she believed in being a good sport in return.

"Everything is fine," she typed. "Don't worry about all the rumors, Broadway's full of them! AURORA is still here and still going strong, see you tomorrow at eight!"

As she sat there, the comments and questions kept piling up on the *Aurora* blog, and Marlena finally allowed herself to wonder: *Is it us?* Could *Aurora* be closing? There'd been rumors before, but never anything like this.

She looked around her lovely two-bedroom apartment on Riverside Drive, with its view of the Hudson River. Marlena had been shaking her booty in low-budget music videos when she'd gotten plucked out of an open call to star in this show.

Now she had an agent, a manager, a lawyer, a stylist, and a life coach who'd been meditating with her once a week to "gain clarity" on her next career move.

Unless I already blew it, she thought anxiously. Her manager already had clarity; he'd been killing himself getting the big record companies interested in her, but six months ago her theatre agent had urged her to renew her contract with *Aurora* and she had. Now she was stuck for a year, and even after all that meditating she still wasn't sure she'd made the right choice.

"*Beyoncé!*" her manager had yelled, furious, when he found out what she'd done. "*J Lo!* They make a lot more money than you do, little Miss Broadway Star!" It was true, but how did you walk away from a dream? Marlena had wanted to be on Broadway since she was a little girl taking tap in the Kingsbridge section of the Bronx, and now she was going to quit?

She thought of her boy band costar. Nice kid, pretty hair, not much voice but that's what microphones were for. He was doing *Aurora* on the advice of his agents, to shake up his image so he could make the transition to feature films.

"He's a *bankable star,*" Marlena's manager had said sternly, when she'd first complained about having to work with Mr. Pretty Hair, who didn't know stage right from stage left. "That's what *you* need to become, Marlena Ortiz!"

She looked at her smiling face on the screen, an airbrushed memento of her former naïveté. The public always thought the actors were the big deal, but Marlena knew better. The real power in the theatre was not onstage but in windowed offices and wood-paneled conference rooms, with the producers and directors, the ad agencies and critics and investors.

And the writers, she thought. But Marlena didn't know who'd written *Aurora.* She'd been given a phone number on the first day of rehearsals. "In case you have any questions about the role, and the director is unavailable, call and leave a message here and someone will call you back." That's what the stage manager had told her.

She'd only called the number once, after the opening-night party when she was a little tipsy and feeling fine. She'd left a message saying congratulations and asking whoever it was out on a date, just for fun. After that she was told not to call except in an emergency.

But now something was up, and she'd be damned if Marlena Ortiz was going to be the last person to know what it was. If *Aurora* was closing, she needed to get her manager back on the phone with RCA, today. It wasn't too late to plan a fall concert tour, but first she needed to get in the studio and lay down the album they'd been talking about before she renewed her contract with *Aurora.*

Emergency? I'll make it an emergency, she thought, and picked up the phone.

"It's only five paragraphs, you can do it!" Philip was trying to be encouraging, but Emily's writer's block had reached crisis proportions and he was nearly out of patience. It was study hall for both of them, and they sat at adjacent computers in the school library. Philip had found a helpful Web site that gave sample outlines and topics for persuasive essays, and Emily was staring at a blank screen, freaking out.

"Henderson's class starts in thirty minutes," she said anxiously. "That's six minutes a paragraph."

"Too bad it's not a math class," Philip joked, but she didn't seem to get it. He turned back to the screen. "How about one of these topics? School uniforms, yes or no? Capital punishment, yes or no? Violence in the media, harmless or the end of civilization? Hey, here's an easy one: which make better pets: cats or dogs?"

"You know I'm allergic to fur," Emily said. "Look! Oh my God, twenty-nine minutes."

"Pick anything!" he urged. "Better to turn in a bad paper than blow off the assignment and get a zero averaged into your grade."

"My topic: Why RuneScape is dumb!" Emily snarled pointedly. A bunch of goth gamer kids were hovering around waiting for the computers, but since Emily and Philip were attempting to do actual schoolwork, the massively multiplayer crowd had to wait.

"Eat me," one of them snarled, but they backed off.

Philip looked at the retreating mob and let their wardrobe choices inspire him. "School uniforms, then," he suggested to Emily. "You can't be allergic to them."

"If they're wool I am," Emily said. "Twenty-eight minutes! What am I gonna do what am I gonna do—"

"Just write something. Anything!"

"Okay! I'm just gonna write anything."

"Good."

"Shhh!" Her eyes were closed and her fingers hammered at the keys. "Don't talk to me. I'm writing."

Good, he almost said, but stopped himself. Highly practiced at making it look like he was doing something educational when he was, in fact, surfing the theatre chat rooms, Philip quickly logged on to planetbroadway.com. Somebody IM'd him almost immediately.

SAVEMEFROMAURORA: Hey, isn't it a school day?

SAVEMEFROMAURORA: Aren't you supposed to be coloring inside the lines right about now?

BwayPhil: Well, hello there.

BwayPhil: We're in the school library, it's study hall.

BwayPhil: Aurorarox is sitting next to me.

SAVEMEFROMAURORA: Hi 'rox.

BwayPhil: She would say hi but she's trying to finish a paper.

"Oh God," Emily moaned, typing away. "Twenty minutes! That's four minutes a paragraph. . . ."

SAVEMEFROMAURORA: Are you following all the rumors? The Internuts are having a field day.

BwayPhil: Somewhat, yes.

BwayPhil: I guess people who like to gossip will always find something to gossip about.

SAVEMEFROMAURORA: You don't sound too interested. I'll keep my scoop to myself then. . . .

"Pompous jerk," Philip said under his breath.

"Who's that?" Emily asked.

"Just write, okay?"

"Rrrrr." But she went back to work.

BwayPhil: Why, what have you heard?

SAVEMEFROMAURORA: Just what everybody's heard. That something's closing.

SAVEMEFROMAURORA: 'cept I know what, tee hee.

BwayPhil: Do you really?

BwayPhil: Because it would be really mean and f***ed up for you to play with our heads.

SAVEMEFROMAURORA: Wouldn't it, though? Lucky for you I'm actually a nice person, in my fashion.

SAVEMEFROMAURORA: And yes, I do know. Really.

"Hey, Em." Philip spoke in a calm voice, suitable for libraries but totally unsuited to the import of what was happening on the screen. "You better come here."

"Not now!" She looked at the clock. "I have fifteen minutes to write a five-paragraph essay. That's three minutes a paragraph."

"It's SAVEME. He says he knows what's closing."

Emily spun around in her chair and all her notebooks fell to the ground.

SAVEMEFROMAURORA: Still there, Bway?

BwayPhil: Yes, sorry. Are you going to tell us which show?

SAVEMEFROMAURORA: It's one of 'em.

SAVEMEFROMAURORA: Ask me too many questions and I'll say no more.

Philip looked up at Emily, who was digging her fingers into his shoulder so hard it hurt.

"Don't ask him anything," she whispered.

Philip let his hands hover over the keyboard for a long minute before entering his reply.

BwayPhil: Notice how we are asking no questions at all.

SAVEMEFROMAURORA: The silence was deafening, good boy. Now listen closely, only saying this once:

SAVEMEFROMAURORA: If I were you I'd go see your favorite show again soon.

BwayPhil: Why?

Emily punched Philip in the shoulder. "He said not to ask him any more questions!" she hissed.

"Wait, he's typing," Philip said.

SAVEMEFROMAURORA: That's not for me to discuss. Just go. Buy the tickets today if you can.

BwayPhil: Today? What are you saying, SAVEME?—

SAVEMEFROMAURORA: Saying nothing, just a hunch is all—

"I would really love to sock this guy in the face," muttered Philip as he typed.

BwayPhil: This IS NOT a question, but does the magic 8 ball have an ***opinion*** about which perf we should buy tix for?

SAVEMEFROMAURORA: Saturday night, two weeks from now would be ideal.

SAVEMEFROMAURORA: Or anytime before.

SAVEMEFROMAURORA: This is just a hunch, remember. Don't go spreading it around like cream cheese.

BwayPhil: So why are you telling us?

SAVEMEFROMAURORA: Truthfully?

SAVEMEFROMAURORA: Let's just say I had to tell somebody,

SAVEMEFROMAURORA: and I don't have many friends.

BwayPhil: Aurorarox losing mind now and insisting I let her—

BwayPhil: rox typing now as BPhil—hey, saveme?

SAVEMEFROMAURORA: yezzz, 'rox?

BwayPhil: i thought you were a jerk

SAVEMEFROMAURORA: But you were wrong.

BwayPhil: right

SAVEMEFROMAURORA: 'pology accepted, Roxie—hang on, phone's a-ringing—

BwayPhil: can you at least tell us how you know—?
SAVEMEFROMAURORA: Gotta take this call, bye sports fans.
BwayPhil: ok
BwayPhil: thanx for the hunch, saveme

"Oh my God, Phil." Emily never called him Phil but it just came out. "Oh my God oh my God."

"What do you think?" asked Philip. "Do you think he's telling the truth?"

"Close your eyes," she said, taking both his hands in hers, just the way Aurora did to Enrique in the second act of *Aurora*. "Look into your heart. True or not true?"

They looked into their hearts. Then they looked at each other. They'd both gotten the same answer.

"True," Emily whispered. "What are we going to do?"

Her question was rhetorical, but Philip chose to answer it as a practical matter. "Here's exactly what we're going to do," he said. "We are going into the city *today* to buy tickets. We are going to have to pay full price to buy in advance, so we'll need quite a bit of money."

Emily was nodding, but her head was swirling with numbers. "Two weeks. Sixteen shows. Sixteen pairs of tickets, a hundred dollars each."

"Em," he said, alarmed. "That's thirty-two hundred dollars."

"I want to see them all," she said, her voice cracking. "Every show that's left. I have to. *I have to*. I'll ask Grandma Rose for it, she'll understand."

"It's an awful lot of money—"

"You have to see your show while it's running! Isn't that what she always says?" Emily felt the hysteria climbing up from her gut.

"It is, but still—"

"So that's what we'll do." Her mind was made up. "And we will see the show as many times as we can between now and— and—"

Emily couldn't say it.

Two weeks from Saturday. It sounded so incredibly soon. Tears started to roll down Emily's cheeks, and Philip reacted in the only way he could think of.

He sang to her, softly, so as not to anger the librarian.

> *"Forever will have to be enough,*
> *Not one day less will do,*
> *But forever could never be enough,*
> *To celebrate all my love—"*

For you were the lyrics that ended the song, but Philip didn't go quite that far. He looked at his watch instead. "The box office opens at three—that means we have to make the one-forty-eight train."

"First we have to stop at my house and get the money," Emily said. "Let's go."

"Emily, what about your persuasive essay?" Philip said. "You should turn it in, at least."

Honestly, Emily thought, *did Sweeney Todd pause to turn in his homework before slitting someone's throat with a razor?* How sadly unlike a musical her life too often was. Perhaps she should do something about that.

"Prepare," said Emily, "for my greatest performance to date."

13

"AND I AM TELLING YOU"

Dreamgirls
**1981. Music by Henry Krieger,
lyrics and book by Tom Eyen**

Emily grabbed her persuasive essay from the printer—God only knew what she'd written, she didn't even bother to read it over—and raced, only a few minutes late, to Mr. Henderson's class. She slapped the paper on his desk and slid into the nearest empty seat.

"Emily Pearl! Give me an example of *literary symbolism*," Mr. Henderson said. He had a very resonant voice. Emily thought it would be a good voice for an actor, assuming Mr. Henderson had any talent.

"The great white way," she said, with hardly a moment's hesitation. "From *Moby-Dick*."

Emily was surprised to hear titters from her classmates.

"Really?" Mr. Henderson was far from the meanest teacher

at Eleanor Roosevelt, but Emily knew he wasn't above using sarcasm as a teaching tool, either. "The Great White Way is a nickname for Broadway, Emily. Broadway—perhaps you've heard of it? I believe they have *musicals* there?"

"I meant whale," Emily said, annoyed. Obviously she'd meant whale; what was he, stupid? "Way, whale. Whatever."

"Ah, *whale*. That's better. Thank you, Emily." Mr. Henderson continued his lecture about symbolism, and Emily snuck a look at her watch. It was 12:55. She took a few deep breaths and let out a soft moan, but no one noticed.

"I have an idea," said Mr. Henderson. "I'll throw an A, weighted as a quiz, into this marking period's average for the first person who can tell me the correct etymology of the phrase 'Great White Way' as a nickname for Broadway."

Emily moaned loader. Then she winced and raised her hand.

"What's the matter, Emily?" Mr. Henderson said. "Don't tell me you have the answer already? Or perhaps"—and here he turned to the class—"you're going to ask me what 'etymology' means?"

Emily willed her face to go pale. "Sorry, Mr. Henderson," she said, in a tremulous voice. "I need to be excused. I think I'm going to—to—"

She gagged. She leapt to her feet, swayed drunkenly, and clutched the desk for support. Nearby students recoiled in horror.

Then Emily clapped her hand over her mouth and ran out the door of the classroom. Not a single person tried to stop her.

"Grandma? Grandma Rose?"

Emily and Philip stood in the doorway of the tidy downstairs bedroom. It hadn't occurred to Emily that Grandma

Rose might not be home. Was Monday the day she had lunch at the diner with her girlfriends? Had she mentioned a doctor's appointment? Emily wished she paid more attention to these things.

"My mom usually leaves some grocery money. We could take that," Philip said nervously, knowing it might not even be enough for one pair of tickets.

"I know where she keeps her cash." She moved to the dresser. "I'm sure she won't mind. I'll just leave a note."

Emily tried not to look as she opened Grandma Rose's underwear drawer, gingerly pushing aside some lacy black garments to find the wooden cigar box. She opened it and quickly counted.

"Two thousand dollars." Emily was determined. "It's not enough, but it'll do."

"Could we at least call her or something?" Philip asked. Standing in the Pearls' empty house and taking Grandma Rose's money without permission was feeling very, very wrong to him. On the other hand, Philip was a person who lived with both a purveyor of fake IDs and (when she was home) a lawyer, so he was used to moral uncertainty.

Emily was already writing. "It'll be fine," she said through her teeth.

Dear Grandma Rose,

I'm so sorry I didn't get to ask you in advance, but I know you won't mind. There's an emergency with "my show," and I have to go buy tickets today or I'll never see it again! Think of Zero Mostel and you'll understand.

I have taken the remaining cash from your

cigar box. Hope I didn't mess up the drawer too much!

I really, really, REALLY appreciate all the money you've lent me and as soon as I get hold of my "college" money I will pay you back.

Your loving granddaughter
(& fellow theatre lover),
Em

Even with Philip standing and pedaling Emily's bike like a madman and Emily hunched down and clutching the seat in the most aerodynamic position she could manage without falling off, they barely made it to the train station in time. When they arrived, the warning *clang-clang-clang* was sounding and the train was already within view, huffing and whistling into the station, so they didn't even have time to lock Emily's bike to the bike rack.

If it's gone when we get back, it's gone, Emily thought as they raced up the stairs to the platform. She'd walk home if she had to. She couldn't very well ask her parents to pick her up at the train station. *No, nothing's wrong, I just cut school and stole money from Grandma's room and went to the city without permission, so can you pick me up?*

Of course, if the bike was stolen that too would require a story of some kind—*I'll tell them it was stolen from school,* she thought—but then they might feel it necessary to call the principal and file some sort of report. She still hadn't decided how she was going to justify her absence from the dinner table tonight, though she could always call and say she was eating at Philip's. But what about all the nights to come over the next two weeks, when she'd be seeing *Aurora* again and again and again?

Emily looked at Philip with envy. He never had to lie, because nobody in his family paid attention to anything he did. Emily had a fleeting wish that she were an orphan (not a real one, with dead parents or anything like that, of course, but a cute singing-and-dancing orphan, like from *Annie* or *Oliver!*). Or away at college, where she could come and go without this constant explaining, explaining, explaining.

College! Would she have enough money to pay for it, after all she'd spent on *Aurora* tickets? She'd never bothered to add it up—

"All aboard!" the conductor yelled, waving them onto the train. "Move it, move it!"

Two thousand dollars. Ten pairs of tickets. It would be a final fling, a Broadway binge, a two-week *Aurora* spree paid for with ill-gotten funds and concealed with lies, but that's the way the Aurorafans of Rockville Centre intended to go down: in flames, like Roxie Hart and Velma Kelly from *Chicago*, or any of those other infamous criminal partnerships that ended in a defiant, musical bloodbath as the lights faded to black.

If my life were a musical, Philip thought, *the next two weeks would be one of those elaborate sung sequences where a lot of time passes in the course of a single number.*

There were many examples of this kind of number, but his favorite was in the second act of *Gypsy*, after awkward, shy Louise is pushed unwillingly onto the stage by her ferociously ambitious mother, Rose. Louise starts out an awkward teen, nervously singing "Let Me Entertain You" to a crowd of catcalling men, yet with every cross of the stage she gains confidence until finally she's transformed into the legendary stripper Gypsy Rose Lee. All in a single song! How did musicals do that?

First refrain: Philip and Emily are nervously buying tickets

97

at the box office, pushing that big wad of bills through the little hole in the box office window.

Second refrain: Now they are blithe ticket holders, sauntering past their former rush line peers and greeting the ushers by name.

Third refrain: Caution is thrown to the winds! They see the show from every vantage point. From high up they look into the orchestra pit and wave at the brass players, who wave back. From all the way left or right they catch glimpses of the actors in the wings just before they make their entrances, nervously stretching and swigging from their water bottles and trying to make the onstage actors laugh by arranging themselves into ludicrous tableaux.

The finale: A madcap montage of Emily and Philip seeing *Aurora,* again and again and again. They skip school and spend every day in the city hanging around the theatre, soaking it all up, missing nothing. Mrs. Nebbling never notices Philip's absence, and the Pearls—

"Em—" Philip said, dropping abruptly back into reality. They were about to enter the tunnel to Penn Station; out the window he could see Long Island City's tall, gleaming Citibank building looming ahead of them, as if Queens were giving Manhattan the finger. "What are you going to tell your parents?"

Emily smiled a mischievous smile. "I just figured it out," she said. "I'm going to tell them I got into the show."

"What—you mean *Aurora?*" Emily could carry a tune, sort of, but surely her parents were not that gullible.

"*Fiddler on the Roof,*" Emily explained. "At school! I'll be the third peasant from the left. Rehearsals every night and all day Saturday. It's the perfect excuse."

It was, he had to admit, but there was one flaw in her plan. "Won't they want to come see it, though?" he asked. "You'll be totally busted when they notice you're not in it."

Emily pointed at her throat. "Laryngitis," she wheezed dramatically. "It'll hit me right before opening night. What a shame."

The two of them laughed very, very hard at that.

Despite the urgency of their mission, Philip and Emily walked calmly, in a nearly normal fashion, from the Forty-second Street subway stop, past the usual array of handbag vendors and hot dog carts and apocalyptic preachers, all plying their trades beneath the cacophony of billboards and looming JumboTrons of Times Square.

Something was bothering Philip. Not Ian; he and Emily had resolved that ethical dilemma already. They knew Ian was in nonstop rehearsals for a show at LaGuardia and wouldn't be available to see *Aurora* for the next two weeks anyway. Breaking their "don't tell" promise to SAVEME would make no practical difference in Ian's case. Besides, Ian was a rush line friend, not a friend friend. The strict no-cutting-and-no-holding-places-for-friends ethos of the line seemed to apply here.

As for Stephanie . . . well, what could they do? It was horrifying that you could be in a show and not realize it was about to close, but in Stephanie's case it was a professional matter and they hardly knew her well enough to interfere. That was Emily's argument, anyway, and Philip went along, though he did feel sorry for Stephanie. *No wonder actors are obsessed with gossip,* he thought. *Their jobs could be on the line.*

No, what was bothering Philip had to do with him and

Emily, and he had to say it before they got to the box office. He sucked up his courage and blurted it out.

"You don't have to buy tickets for me, you know."

"What?" Emily said, genuinely surprised.

His voice stuck in his throat. "With this money you could go to all sixteen performances yourself and still have enough—" He was going to say "to take me four times," but he didn't. Seeing *Aurora* four times in two weeks would be twice as much *Aurora* as he was used to; it should have felt like a lot, but the rhythm of his heart was beating *Four times will never be enough, never be enough, never be enough.* If only he had some money of his own—a college fund to borrow against, a grandma to float him a loan, a second parent to help support the family, pancakes for breakfast instead of cold pizza or sometimes nothing . . .

Emily, meanwhile, was reeling. The option of going to the show by herself had simply not occurred to her before, but now, of course, it had. Talk about an ethical dilemma!

If my life were a musical, Emily thought in a rush, *I would do what Aurora would do,* and before she could change her mind she said, "I would not want to go without you, Philip."

It sounded incredible. It sounded like the kind of thing someone would say right before bursting into song.

"Emily, don't be dumb," Philip said bravely. "Of course you should go."

"And I am telling you, I'm not going," Emily said, straight-faced.

"*Dreamgirls.*" Philip looked deep into her eyes. "1981. Music by Henry Krieger, book and lyrics by Tom Eyen."

Emily grinned, though she felt shaky inside. "It wasn't a show question," she said. It was 2:43, and they were about to make their final approach to the Rialto Theatre.

★   ★   ★

Philip had made a last sweep of the Broadway message boards as well as the official *Aurora* blog before leaving the school library, and though the morning's Internut rumors had grown both more numerous and more outlandish—the idea of *Beauty and the Beast* closing to make room for a musical version of *Napoleon Dynamite* seemed farfetched, even by Broadway logic—none of the rank-and-file gossipmongers was pinpointing *Aurora* as the show whose head was on the block. As far as Philip and Emily knew, they, Lester, and apparently SAVEME were the only people who knew—or at least, believed—that *Aurora* was closing.

"Do you think," Emily asked as they turned the corner of Broadway and West Forty-fourth Street, "that SAVEME could *be* Lester?"

"Huh," said Philip. "That kinda makes sense, actually. How could we find out?"

"We'll ask Ian to tell us something about Lester, some personal detail, and then we can—we can—" But the words died in her mouth.

It was 2:45. The box office opened in fifteen minutes, and the mob scene outside the theatre extended all the way down Forty-fourth Street to Eighth Avenue and who knew how far around the block.

Stupefied, speechless, they froze in midstep. Emily started to totter on her feet and grabbed Philip's arm.

Something has gone wrong, so very, very wrong, thought Philip. Reflexively he tried to quantify the disaster—three, four, five hundred people, he guessed, with streams of newcomers arriving by the minute. And that wasn't counting the unseen hordes on Eighth Avenue.

"Can you believe it!" screamed Daphne, the costumed

rush line regular. She waved her funky knit scarf in the air like a flag as she spotted them. "Can you believe it can you believe it can you believe it!"

Maybe Daphne was repeating herself, or maybe sounds were echoing inside Emily's head. She couldn't tell; nor could she tell if she was pulling Philip over to where Daphne was standing—there seemed to be an actual line snaking through the mob, and Daphne was on it—or if Philip was pulling her.

"Oh my God I can't stand it I can't stand it I can't stand it," Daphne was saying. "I can't believe *Aurora* is closing!"

Hearing Daphne say it aloud made something inside Emily's head pop, like her ears did on planes during takeoff. "Where did you hear that?" she demanded, hanging on to Philip for dear life and trying not to shriek. "Who told you that?"

"Who told me is the same person who told everybody here!" cried Daphne, gesturing dramatically with her fuzzy *Aurora*-style mittens. "She posted it on the *Aurora* blog about"—Daphne pushed up one mitten so she could see her watch—"an hour ago."

"An hour ago?" Philip repeated. "An hour—"

"Who?" screamed Emily. "Who who who who?"

Daphne looked at them, dumbfounded. "Marlena!" she said. "Marlena Ortiz!"

14

"I BELIEVE IN YOU"

How to Succeed in Business
Without Really Trying
**1961. Music and lyrics by Frank Loesser,
book by Abe Burrows, Jack Weinstock, and Willie Gilbert**

Philip and Emily gaped at each other. An hour ago—that would have been right about the time Emily was faking a puke attack in Mr. Henderson's class, the same time that Philip, who hadn't bothered to show up at his social studies class at all, was sitting in the IHOP across the street from Eleanor Roosevelt High School, waiting for Emily and drinking watery coffee and staring at the train schedule even though he knew it by heart.

Why, Philip thought bitterly, *why couldn't they have wireless Internet access on the Long Island Rail Road, would that be so frickin' hard?*

Daphne looked at them with pity. "Oh my God! You mean you didn't know?"

Emily's stomach gave a little twist. "Of course we knew," she heard herself say. Truthfully, until that minute some secret part of her had clung to the possibility that it was all just noxious gossip, spread, perhaps, by the cast of some competing show, or a publicist for *Wicked* like Ian had said. The stomach pain was spreading upward, into her chest.

Philip looked at Emily, who was wheezing in an asthma-attack kind of way, though he knew she didn't have asthma. He put his hand on her shoulder, to steady both of them.

Data, numbers, facts, figures. That's what Philip needed. Then he would know what to do. "What did Marlena's post say?" he asked Daphne. "Did she say why the show was closing? Did she say when?"

"She was pissed! She was filled with righteousness!" Daphne cried. "She said the producers made the decision to close and didn't even tell Marlena or anyone! They were trying to keep it secret—they thought if Marlena knew, she would walk! As if Marlena Ortiz would ever walk out on *Aurora*! As *if*!" Daphne yelled it to the skies.

The line moved forward an infinitesimal amount. Philip looked at his watch. It was three o'clock. The box office had just opened.

"But Marlena found out somehow—you know Marlena!—and she was like, no way José!" Daphne continued, wagging her finger the way Marlena always did in the first-act finale, in a song titled "You Gotta Show the Love." " 'The fans need to know so they can come show the love,' that's what Marlena said! So she posted it on the blog right away. I guess word got around fast. I ran right outta my office when I saw it. I'm gonna lose my job over this one." Daphne closed her eyes and began to sing.

> "*Show it show it show it show it,*
> *Show the love,*
> *You gotta show it show it show it show it,*
> *Show the love,*
> *You gotta show the love!*"

Daphne started to sway as she sang.

Though she loved every syllable and every note of every song from *Aurora*, hearing Daphne sing "Show the Love" under these circumstances made Emily want to smack her. "Did she say when the final show is?" Emily yelled, rather close to Daphne's face. Five hundred (or more) people standing in a mob were making a fearsome background noise.

Daphne opened her eyes. "Two weeks from Saturday," she said. "You better get on the back of the line, girl, there is no way we're all gonna get tickets!" Daphne draped her scarf across her face like a veil and started dancing. "I heard they're only letting each person buy two."

"Philip!" Emily said, her voice rising with panic. "Did you hear that?"

Of course he had. His mind was already calculating—two weeks, sixteen performances. It was reasonable to assume the roughly 1,500-seat theatre was presold for say, seventy percent of the tickets, leaving approximately 450 seats unsold for each performance, for a total of 7,200 available seats—but Aurora-fans everywhere were working their telephones and computers this very second, gobbling up the remaining *Aurora* tickets on Telecharge, while he and Emily stood here, not even in line yet and with throngs of people already waiting. . . .

It was hopeless. Philip had two thousand dollars cash in his pocket (Emily had been too nervous to carry it), but you had to have a credit card to use Telecharge. They could walk up the line trying to scalp tickets for crazy amounts of money, but the hard-core *Aurora* crowd despised scalpers; if he started to flash his cash they might end up being stoned to death, or (the New York version) being pushed in front of a speeding taxi. . . .

"Please, Daphne, let us stand here with you!" Emily begged. "We were on the train and we didn't see Marlena's post, we just got here, you know we would have been the first ones here if we'd known—"

A warning grumble started to rise from the people in line behind Daphne, but they needn't have worried. "I'm sorry, honey," Daphne said, shaking her head. "But justice is justice, I can't mess with the way things are meant to be." She started singing a different *Aurora* song:

> *"Look inside!*
> *See what you see.*
> *Who you are*
> *Is who you're meant to be—"*

Philip, meantime, was counting heads. There were now close to seven hundred people clamoring for tickets. There was only one thing to do.

"Hey!" said Daphne as Philip started to lead Emily away. "If you didn't know about Marlena's post, how did you find out the show was closing?"

"We uh, uh, uh—" said Emily.

"Emily, let's go," said Philip, gently tugging her arm. "We have to get in line."

Upstairs in the Sardi's building on West Forty-fourth Street, Stevie Stephenson looked out the windowed rear wall of his office. The floor-to-ceiling glass offered a heart-stopping view of Times Square: the animated advertisements, the glittering theatre marquees, not to mention the underwear models pictured on Times Square's legendary sky-high billboards. From each photo a tanned and oiled, nearly naked model gazed moodily into Stevie's tenth-floor office. It made his visitors uncomfortable, and Stevie liked that.

Ten stories down, on street level—Stevie liked what he saw there, too. The theatre district was always crowded, but the sea of desperate ticket-buying humanity before him triggered a special thrill in his nervous system. He lived by the producers' credo, also known as PBIS: Put Butts In Seats. Most of the people on the street below had never heard of Stevie Stephenson, but at this moment he was a man who wielded power over an awful lot of butts.

One of the nicest of these belonged to Marlena Ortiz, and Stevie chuckled at how well his little plan had worked. How easy it had been to let his news about *Aurora* "slip" to his idiot nephew Lester in Florida. How quickly the "rumor," thus carefully planted, had spread, finding its way back to the intended target within a twenty-four-hour period and leaving a comet-trail of gossip (and free publicity!) a mile wide.

He still wasn't sure how Marlena had gotten to the heart of the rumor and confirmed it so quickly, but it didn't matter. Her reaction was perfect: utterly predictable and endearingly, wrongheadedly noble. Three years of playing *Aurora* had turned the wide-eyed chorus girl into not merely a star, but one who fancied herself a "woman of the people"—it was touching, really, the way she took her fans so seriously.

She'd make a fine Evita someday, he mused. For now, Marlena had done for free what a thousand highly paid press agents couldn't—she'd turned an ordinary closing notice into a phenomenon.

And just wait, he thought. *Wait till you hear what's coming to the Rialto next.*

The One Sure Thing in Show Business, that's what. He had two signed contracts as proof, typed very late at night by a specially hired temp who could input a hundred words a minute but understood not one word of English. Stevie knew how to leak a secret, and he also knew how to keep one.

The One Sure Thing in Show Business. Steve smiled. All the top producers knew what it was, but none of them—so far— had been able to make the deal happen. To do so would be like catching lightning in a bottle. Many said it was impossible and had given up trying. Not Stevie.

He grabbed a stick of cinnamon gum from his desk drawer. Stevie had quit smoking cigars a decade earlier on the advice of his doctor, but at times like this he would get a craving.

Music, he thought as he chewed. That's what he needed. He punched the intercom button on his desk.

"Miss O'Malley," he said. "Would you put on the *How to Succeed in Business Without Really Trying* recording, and pipe it in to my office?"

"Original cast with Robert Morse, or 1995 revival with Matthew Broderick?" asked Miss O'Malley, without missing a beat.

"Matthew Broderick." Stevie snapped his gum with satisfaction. "Broderick, please."

It was two full hours before word got down to the end of the line, transmitted from person to person like an evil game of telephone—there were no more tickets. The box office was closing. Everyone should go home.

By this time Emily and Philip had about two hundred people in line behind them and six hundred people still in front. For the last half hour Philip's teeth had been chattering and Emily had needed to go to the bathroom, but they had stood resolutely, without complaining.

They'd passed so many familiar faces on their long walk to the end of the line—it seemed like most of the regulars were there. Some waved, others averted their eyes. From a half block away Morris had mouthed, "You just GOT here?" in disbelief before limping off into the crowd. None of them had offered to let Emily and Philip cut the line, but if they had it might have started a riot, so it was just as well.

There were no more tickets. The box office was closing. Everyone should go home.

Somebody nearby started to cry. Others stood there, unable to leave the line, but no longer knowing what they were waiting for. After a few minutes, the bulk of the crowd wandered off in defeat. One group started singing as they walked away:

> *"Never be enough*
> *Ten thousands shows could*
> *Never be enough . . ."*

But Emily and Philip, the die-hard Aurorafans of Rockville Centre, could not leave without some final heroic effort, no matter how futile. Without even needing to discuss it, they ran, weaving at full speed through the thinning crowd, to the Rialto Theatre box office. The manager was about to turn out the lights.

"Please!" Emily cried, pounding on the box office window. "We *have* to have tickets to the final performance! You can charge us anything you want. We'll stand in the back. We'll watch from the wings!"

The box office manager looked exhausted. Grimacing, he said to Emily what he'd already gone hoarse saying to 426 people before her, not that any of them had believed him, either.

"Regardless of what you may have read on the Internet, 'officially' we have not announced a closing," he croaked. "So 'officially' there is no final performance!" He started to pull down the Plexiglas divider that shut the box office window.

"But unofficially?" Emily cried, jamming her hand under the glass. The manager was barely able to stop the window before it smashed into her fingers.

"Unofficially—the next two weeks are completely sold out. We're not selling tickets for performances after that date at this time." He looked at them with burning eyes. "Do I have to write it in blood? Go home!"

"Wait!" said Philip. "Will there be any rush lines on the days of performance?"

"No more rush lines!" The box office manager put his mouth right next to the narrow opening beneath the glass. Emily could feel his breath on her hand. "There are no more tickets!" he rasped. "Got it? Go see *Phantom of the Opera*! This box office is closed."

Emily barely got her fingers out before he slammed the window shut.

15

"KEEP IT GAY"

The Producers
**2001. Music and lyrics by Mel Brooks,
book by Mel Brooks and Thomas Meehan**

There are times when a person is alone in her room crying but is secretly hoping someone will come in and find her, sit on the side of the bed, ask the right questions and listen calmly, all while radiating a tender glow of sympathy and understanding.

This was not a time like that. This was a time when Emily wanted more than anything to hide from the truth, pull the blankets over her feelings and pretend that everything, just for a moment, was the way it used to be. But her feelings refused to cooperate. They erupted, hot as lava, and poured down her cheeks and twisted her face into a horrible tight crying expression that made her feel like her skin would split.

She'd slept on and off all night, waking, remembering, crying, dozing, and waking again. Her bike had been gone from the train station when she and Philip got back, as she'd expected, but that didn't make it any less upsetting. Luckily her parents had been too distracted by the missing bike to poke any serious holes in her story about the PSAT class instructor being late and taking the class out for pizza afterward to make amends.

Grandma Rose had been out for the evening and had uncharacteristically left the door to her room locked, so the unspent two thousand dollars (minus the cab fare from the station) was stashed in Emily's closet, rolled inside a bedroom slipper and hidden in the back, behind her summer clothes.

Emily thought of all these things during her wakeful fits of misery, but mostly she thought of *Aurora*.

Is this how things ended? she'd wondered at 3:18 a.m., when she finally left her bed and stared out the bedroom window at the street below. *With the last time of whatever it was you loved already over, and you didn't know it was the last time so you didn't pay special attention or say goodbye or anything?*

If that was what last times felt like, she realized with horror, *anything* could be the last time. This could be the last time Emily stood shivering in front of her window, or the last night she spent in her own bed.

Maybe a meteor would strike her house this minute and crush them all to powder, making this the last time she'd be able to think about what last times felt like!

Emily remembered her bike—she'd never ride it again, *never never never*—and started to cry again. She crawled back under the covers and hugged her pillow, until she dozed off once more.

Much to his surprise, Philip woke up on Tuesday morning to the smell of pancakes.

For a moment he wondered if he might be having a stroke. That was a symptom of stroke—you started to smell things that weren't there. He was sure he'd read something like that in a book once. He inhaled. Pancakes. A stroke, definitely.

Even after going to the bathroom and splashing water on his face he smelled it, and as he approached the kitchen he heard something sizzle, just like batter on a hot griddle. Obviously the stress of *Aurora*'s closing had caused some fragile artery in his brain to weaken and burst—

"Good morning, honey!" said Mrs. Nebbling. She was wearing not her customary hazmat suit, but an apron, and she was cooking breakfast. "I decided to stay home today."

"Oh. Hey." Philip wondered if he should kiss her on the cheek, but she was holding a drippy ladle in one hand and a greasy spatula in the other. It seemed dangerous to get too close.

"I'm making breakfast," she said.

"Yeah," said Philip. "I smelled it. I thought it was a stroke."

"What?" she asked.

"Nothing," said Philip, peering at the griddle. "That batch needs to be flipped."

"I'm so sorry I wasn't home for your birthday," she said. "I hope you had fun." The kitchen was filling with smoke. If there had been batteries in the alarm, it would have gone off by now.

"It's okay." Philip reached over the stovetop and turned on the exhaust fan.

"Thanks," said Mrs. Nebbling. She handed him a plate of steaming pancakes. "Syrup's on the table."

Philip was so used to eating cold pizza out of the box and Pop-Tarts out of the wrapper, he'd forgotten that the cabinets of the Nebbling kitchen contained actual dishes. Cream-colored background with a pink and green floral pattern around the rim: the same dishes they used to eat dinner off every night in their old house.

"Your brother and I had a long talk last night," Mrs. Nebbling said.

"Mmph," Philip said. The syrup was Mrs. Butterworth's—Philip preferred real maple, which was too expensive for their household now—but the pancakes were delicious. "These are good," he said, his mouth full.

"You look skinny," Mrs. Nebbling said. She smiled at Philip as he ate. It seemed like a fake smile, but maybe Philip had just forgotten what her smile was like. He knew he should be miserable because *Aurora* was closing, but the food tasted so good. Hot breakfast that you ate off a plate! He heard himself making little *yum-yum* noises as he chewed.

"I can understand why you might not have wanted to tell me," Mrs. Nebbling went on. "I haven't been home very much, I know. I guess you probably feel like I'm not interested in your life. But I am."

Philip was distracted by his meal, but not so much that he didn't immediately start to wonder where this was going.

"And don't be mad at Mark," she said. Her smile was starting to look more familiar. "I was the one asking questions. I'm a lawyer, remember?"

Mark is an idiot, Philip wanted to say. *Mark is gross and mean and lies about everything.* But he couldn't say those things because his mouth was crammed full of pancakes.

Mrs. Nebbling put her hand on Philip's, which now bore traces of Mrs. Butterworth's. "Mark told me everything, and I want you to know that I love and accept you exactly the way you are."

"Mark is an idiot," Philip mumbled through his food.

"Philip, honey." Mrs. Nebbling patted his sticky hand. "Mark told me that you're gay."

Emily had never seen her mother so happy.

"A whole season of Matthew Broderick!" Mrs. Pearl squealed. "Oh, Emily! We *have* to get tickets!"

What?

Emily had come downstairs Tuesday morning prepared to smile, to joke, to put on a Tony-worthy performance of acting normal even though her broken heart was imploding like a dying sun, turning its own mass in on itself, collapsing at unfathomable speeds until nothing was left but a black, black, *Aurora*-less hole—but she had no audience.

Mrs. Pearl was completely engrossed in the Tuesday arts section of the paper. "Listen to this, Em! 'Broadway's "Sure Thing" Arrives At Last'! See? It's in the *Times*." Mrs. Pearl pushed the newspaper toward her.

Broadway's "Sure Thing" Arrives At Last

New York—Legendary producer and theatre owner Stevie Stephenson has ended the rumors sweeping theatrical circles in recent days by announcing a full season of plays, musicals and dramatic readings at the Rialto Theatre. In an unprecedented casting coup, all programming to be presented at the Rialto will costar Nathan Lane and Matthew Broderick.

"Nathan Lane *and* Matthew Broderick! From *The Producers*!" Mrs. Pearl exclaimed. "They are so funny!"

Plays under consideration for the so-called "Lanerick Rep" include Beckett's existential laugh-fest *Waiting for Godot*, Shakespeare's *Julius Caesar* (with Lane as the treasonous Brutus and Broderick as Cleopatra's boy toy, Marc Antony), and gender-bending versions of *I Do! I Do!*, *Driving Miss Daisy* and *Antigone* (with Lane as King Creon and Broderick as the spunky heroine of the title). "Classic, contemporary, drama, comedy—it doesn't matter," announced Stephenson at a press conference held at Sardi's restaurant. "You can put those two in anything and it'll be a hit!"

Theatre pundits share Stephenson's confidence. "There's no sure thing in show business," says noted theatre critic John Simon, "except Nathan Lane and Matthew Broderick. Producing a show, any show, with those two in it—it's like printing [expletive] money."

Matthew Broderick? Wasn't he married to Sarah Jessica Parker from *Sex and the City*? Emily's heart started to race. The letters on the page swam and circled in front of her eyes. For this she would lose *Aurora*? For the (expletive) money-printing Lanerick Rep?

"The Rialto," said Mrs. Pearl. "Isn't that where that show you like is playing? *Aurora*? Oh, I hope this doesn't mean it's closing!"

Not surprisingly, the *New York Times* was slightly better informed than Mrs. Pearl.

The theatre's current tenant, Tony winner *Aurora*, will be vacating the Rialto at the end of next week despite vehement protests from its fans. When asked if *Aurora* might be moved to another theatre, Stephenson answered in the negative. "Have you seen it?" he asked one reporter. "The ugliest costumes on Broadway, and I should know! I paid for them!"

"Nathan Lane and Matthew Broderick," sighed Mrs. Pearl, her hand over her heart. "In *Antigone*! Who would guess? Did you see a bunch of college catalogs arrived for you? I put them on the dining room table. College! I can't believe it's here already. . . ."

Oh my God, thought Emily. The unspent two thousand dollars was still jammed inside a bedroom slipper in the back of her closet. She needed to put it back. Maybe Grandma Rose hadn't even seen the note in her underwear drawer yet; that would be best of all.

"Is Grandma up?" Emily asked.

"Not yet. She came in late last night and wouldn't say where she'd been. It's almost like having two teenagers in the house!" Mrs. Pearl glanced at the clock. "Come on, I'll drive you to school. I can't believe those awful kids took your bike."

16

"ROSE'S TURN"

Gypsy
1959. Music by Jule Styne, lyrics by Stephen Sondheim, book by Arthur Laurents

The official notice went up the next day. *Aurora* was closing, and Emily and Philip had no choice at all but to go about their lives. They went to school. They went home. They made a solemn pact to avoid the Broadway message boards and chat rooms because the people who were posting were the ones who'd gotten tickets, and it was just too painful to realize the show was going on without them. (Emily wondered briefly if SAVEME was among those lucky few—but a pact was a pact, and she forced herself to put those thoughts aside.)

They went to each other's houses and listened to the *Aurora* CD together. For a while they concocted elaborate schemes that would, theoretically, allow them to see one last performance—they would disguise themselves as ushers, or sneak backstage through the stage door when the doorman wasn't looking, or ambush Marlena Ortiz after the show and beg like their lives depended on it—but soon they ran out of steam.

If I were Dolly Levi from Hello, Dolly!, Emily thought, *I'd be able to charm the stagehands into letting me see the show from the wings. If I were Auntie Mame, I would lead the cast and audience in a curtain-call parade down Broadway.*

If I were Sweeney Todd, Philip thought, *I'd slash throats until somebody coughed up a pair of decent seats in the front mezzanine.* (Philip's imagination had grown a little bloodthirsty lately, probably because he was so angry at Mark.)

It was no good. Noble sacrifices, last-minute redemptions, outlandish coincidences, and madcap risky schemes that made your wildest dreams come true—these things only happened in musicals.

On Thursday they received an e-mail from Ian:

Mes amis,

Exhaustion! Am in full-time rehearsals for this "infernal" show (that's a hint, but no, Philip, it's not *Damn Yankees*! And don't try to guess because even YOU don't know it, it's some newly minted piece of hoo-hah our director brought in and let me tell you it SUCKS).

Tragic what's happened with *Aurora*. La Divina Stephanie pretends to be dis-

traught but has callbacks up the wazoo,
so shed not a tear.

Miss seeing you both on Saturdays. Maybe
you'll come to my show next week? If so,
wear thigh-high boots so you can wade
through the pretension.

Avec kisses,
I.

On Friday Mr. Henderson gave Emily a D on her persuasive essay. "I fail to see," he wrote in neat red script on the bottom, "how the fact that capital punishment does not act as a deterrent to crime inevitably leads to the conclusion that dogs make better pets than cats. Kudos for finding fresh material, though!"

Grandma Rose had been strangely distracted all week, and when Emily gave her back the money she looked like she was about to say something of huge importance and then changed her mind. But she expressed real sympathy when Emily told her *Aurora* was closing. "Goodbye, Charlie," Grandma Rose said, nodding. "I know how it feels."

Tuesday. Seven performances left.

"Darling! You remember my boyfriend, Stan, don't you?"

Grandma Rose had invited Emily and Philip out for egg creams at the coffee shop on Lakeview Avenue after school. Emily appreciated the gesture, but she was beyond cheering up. They went, though. Grandma Rose had been so incredibly nice about everything all along, and who didn't like egg creams? But Emily hadn't expected Grandma to bring a date.

"Nice to see you again, Emily!" Stan looked vaguely familiar, a short and cheerful old man with a lipless, turtle-like smile and very thick glasses that had a seam across the middle of each lens. He stood up to shake Philip's hand without gaining any significant altitude.

Emily racked her brain. She knew she'd met Stan somewhere, once or twice. She'd assumed he was just another of Grandma Rose's card-game friends. Clearly, she had not been following the plot of her grandmother's life closely enough.

"Remember? Stan was at your bat mitzvah," Grandma Rose prompted. "With his wife."

"God rest her soul," Stan added, before Philip and Emily could jump to the wrong conclusion.

"Poor Dolores," Grandma Rose said as the waitress delivered their egg creams: vanilla for Grandma Rose, chocolate for Emily and Stan. Philip was more of a strawberry man. "She suffered. But she'd be happy for us, no?"

"I doubt it!" laughed Stan. "But I'm happy for us! We're happy for us! That's what matters."

Grandma Rose sipped her drink and now had a neat white milk mustache on her upper lip, just like a kid. "So, darling," she said to Emily. "You know that two thousand dollars I had stashed away? That you borrowed without asking but then gave back immediately, because you're such a fine and up-standing young woman?"

"Yes," said Emily tentatively. "I hope you weren't angry about that! We were kind of desperate."

"Of course I'm not angry! We're family; we're supposed to live out of each other's pockets." Grandma Rose took Stan's hand. "I just wanted to tell you some wonderful news: Stan and I used that money to put a down payment on a sweet Winnebago I found on eBay."

Stan leaned forward conspiratorially. "It's in Weehawken. We gotta give it a test drive, but otherwise it's a done deal."

"You see," Grandma Rose said, "Stan and I are leaving. Keep it under your hats, though. It's a secret."

The unexpected news caught Philip in midslurp. Emily's mouth fell open but nothing came out, at first. "Together?" she said, finally.

"Of course together! Stan is—what do you kids say?" Grandma winked at them. "My main squeeze."

"Nobody says 'main squeeze,' Grandma." Emily moved and almost knocked over her egg cream, but Philip saved it at the last minute. "What do you mean, leaving?"

"Stan's eyesight is going, and his kids want to put him in assisted living." Grandma Rose glanced around and lowered her voice. "So we're running away."

"Assisted living?" asked Philip. "What's that?" The phrase sounded familiar; he thought it might be the title of a Noël Coward play.

"Two meals a day and somebody cleans your room," Stan explained. "Feh. Who wants to live like that? With a bunch of old people?"

Grandma Rose made a wonderfully rude gesture. "Assist this! That's what I say."

To Philip, of course, two meals a day and a clean room sounded great, but he thought it best not to argue.

Grandma dabbed a napkin to her lips. "The thing is, Stan wants to see some things before his eyes go altogether, and I don't blame him."

Stan shrugged. "My kids are busy, working, raising their own kids. They can't drop everything to take me on a world tour."

"The Hanging Gardens of Babylon I can't give him,"

Grandma Rose said, patting his cheek, "but a road trip in a Winnebago I can, and that's what we're gonna do. If we can find the money, that is."

Grandma Rose's statement hung in the air.

How much money exactly has Grandma Rose lent me? Emily thought. It had been what, a little more than a year since she and Philip had started seeing *Aurora* every week? Why hadn't she kept track?

"This Winnebago has Rose and Stan written all over it," Grandma was saying. "I'm afraid we'll lose it if we can't come up with the rest of the cash soon."

How selfish could one person be? A tsunami of guilt washed over Emily. Spending all of Grandma's money on my dreams when she still has dreams of her own . . .

"No, I've never driven a Winnebago, but I rented a U-Haul once," Stan was saying, in response to a question from Philip. "Of course, that was when I could see better."

"Don't worry, I'm doing the driving," Grandma Rose declared. "As long as I don't have to make too many left turns. I hate left turns!"

"You'd be surprised," Stan said, gently putting his arm around Grandma Rose's thin shoulders, "how many places you can get making only right turns." Grandma Rose gazed at him as if they were the only two people on the planet.

They're just like Aurora and Enrique! Emily realized in a flash. *Star-crossed lovers on a last, mad adventure, on the run from impending disability and threats of incarceration . . .*

"I'll get you the money," she blurted out. "All the money you lent me for *Aurora* tickets. I'll get it back for you."

Grandma Rose seemed shocked. Philip looked a little surprised as well.

"Now, honey, where are you gonna get that kind of money?" Grandma Rose said.

"I have it, though, don't I?" Emily asked, in a hopeful voice. "My bat mitzvah money? It's in the bank, for college. That's what you always said."

"Education is very important," Stan observed.

"It certainly is," said Grandma Rose. "Emily is so smart, too. An excellent student."

"The thing is, I'm not really sure how much I owe you, Grandma," Emily said. "I know it's a lot, though."

"Uh, I'm pretty sure I have the figures on that, Em," Philip mumbled. He wasn't sure he should encourage this plan, but it seemed dishonest not to speak up, especially since half of the borrowed money had been spent on him. He wrote a number on a napkin and slid it discreetly in front of Emily.

Emily felt her cheeks grow warm when she saw what Philip had written. It *was* a lot, and she pushed the napkin back to Philip just to be rid of it. "How soon do you need it? The money in this college account—it might take me a while to get it." Truthfully, she didn't have the slightest idea how to withdraw the money, or if she was even entitled to do so.

Grandma Rose thought for a moment. "We should leave for Weehawken before noon tomorrow, don't you think?" she said to Stan. "I don't want this Winnebago to get away."

"Maybe we could go to the bank and just tell them it's yours, Emily." Philip wanted to be helpful, though he had little direct experience with banks.

"What about college?" Stan asked, concerned.

"My Emily is so smart." Grandma Rose beamed. "She'll probably get a scholarship anyway."

"Probably," said Emily, not nearly as confident as her

grandmother. Her grade in Mr. Henderson's class had really tanked this quarter.

"Do what you think is right, darling." Grandma Rose adjusted one of her earrings. "I would never tell you otherwise. Stan and me, we gotta see our show while it's running, you know? That's my motto. Not just for Broadway. For life." She sighed. "Ah, Zero Mostel. Now, *that* was a Tevye."

"Actually," said Philip, "the creators of *Fiddler* have been quoted as saying they preferred Topol; they felt Mostel's performance was over the top and sacrificed the material's integrity for the sake of getting laughs—"

"We'll go to the bank today," said Emily with resolve. Maybe she would never see *Aurora* again, but this, at least— this she could do. And what could be a more fitting tribute to her beloved show?

"We'll give you a lift," said Grandma Rose, reaching for the check. "The egg creams are on me."

I can do this, Emily thought. *I'll do it for Grandma Rose— and for* Aurora.

"It's a five-oh-nine-slash-C fund."

After waiting in line fifteen minutes for a bank teller, Emily had been sent to see a customer service rep. He wore a suit; his neck was bigger than his collar, and his head seemed too big for his face. Emily wondered if perhaps this was why he was in such an unpleasant mood.

"What?"

"A six-oh-four-dash-ninety-nine!" The roll of neck meat that overhung his collar was turning pink. "Tax-deferred!"

Emily twisted and untwisted the straps of her *Aurora* messenger bag. "I'm sorry, I just don't understand."

"Where are you planning to go to college?" the man asked.

"Uh," said Emily. She hated answering this question, because she'd had way too many other things to think about lately besides deciding which college to attend. Yet adults loved to ask. "I was kinda hoping for Yale," she said. It was the first school that came to mind.

"Really," he said. "I'm surprised to hear that. When you get in—*if* you get in—we'll give Yale the money."

"But—"

"It's an education fund, for college tuition only. That's why it's tax-deferred, get it? It's in the tax code, item E-D-forty-nine-point-twelve, paragraphs C through M. Look it up!"

"But I thought it was mine," Emily said weakly. "I mean—that's my bat mitzvah money."

He shook his head, clucking his tongue at her financial ignorance. "It's not yours. It's for the lucky college that takes you. *Yale*, for instance." Was that sarcasm in his voice? He leaned all the way back in his swivel chair, which scrunched his neck even more and made his features seem tiny, like a little Mr. Potato Head face on a really big potato. "Have you ever heard of 'the excesses of youth'?"

Emily shook her head, and he began to explain. "History has proven that unless you earmark these types of accounts for tuition only, young people have a tendency to spend their savings on ephemera."

Ephemera, Emily thought. *Wasn't that the name of the green-skinned witch in* Wicked?

"Fleeting pleasures!" Mr. Potato Head went on. "Fun and games! The triple-Z-sixty-and-three-quarters college fund program prevents that from happening. Who opened this account for you?"

"My dad." Emily sighed. "The excesses of youth"; that was exactly the kind of phrase Mr. Pearl loved to toss around.

"So there *are* some genes for intelligence in your family. Interesting. Yale, huh?" Emily could swear she heard the words "dream on" emanate from the Potato Head man, though his mouth was saying this: "There are plenty of nice state schools, you know. The important thing is to get an education. Practically everyone can be trained to be competent at something." He lifted an eyebrow. "*Practically* everyone."

Philip was still sitting in the bank's waiting area, and he could tell by the look on Emily's face that it hadn't gone well.

"Don't worry," he said, before she even spoke. "We'll go to Plan B."

"Plan B sucks, Philip," Emily said nervously. "Plan B scares me."

"I know," he said. "Me too."

"Tell me the part about the Winnebago again, that *rocks*."

Mark giggled, and Philip wanted to shake him. If only they knew someone else with ready (if ill-gotten) cash and no scruples! Plan B was Mark, and the challenge now was getting their request for a loan through the fog clouding Mark's brain.

"The Winnebago is not important," said Philip impatiently. "Can you lend us the money?"

"The Winnebago is too important, and I will tell you why." Mark shoved half a bag of Doritos in his mouth. "Because I like saying 'Winnebago,' that's why!" He started laughing, revealing the bright orange coating on his teeth and tongue.

Emily looked at Philip questioningly. In the not-unlikely event that Mark started acting like a total freak, Philip and Emily had planned that Emily should burst into tears. Chicks were a vulnerable spot in Mark's personality. He inevitably proved to be a horrendous boyfriend but he honestly adored girls. This gave him a surprising amount of charm with the opposite sex, who in turn had a huge amount of leverage over him.

Philip nodded, and Emily took a tissue out of her pocket, just to be ready. Philip made his final play.

"Listen, Mark," he said. "If you don't want to lend us the money, say so. Then I'll just tell Mom about your little fake ID business and see what happens."

Mark got very sober-looking all at once. "Blackmail is not going to work, so don't even go there, bro."

"Why not?"

"Because you do not have the guts to turn me in. Because it would break your mother's heart. Because she is a lawyer and it could jeopardize her job to have me dragged through the courts." He crumpled the Doritos bag for emphasis. "Because she has enough to deal with, coping with—well, *you* know."

Mark started to "la-la-la" to the tune of "There's No Business Like Show Business." Philip was as livid as he'd ever been in his life. On cue, Emily started to sob, endearingly, convincingly, and Mark's nasty bravado melted into a puddle.

"Why is she crying? What's the matter? What'd I say?" he asked Philip, panicky.

"She's crying because you're a jerk." Philip threw a sock ball at Mark's head. "It's her grandmother we're talking about, get it?"

"Okay, okay now, little girl!" Mark wandered around his chaotically messy side of the bedroom he and Philip shared, looking for tissues, and finally grabbed a roll of paper towels that was lying on top of the dresser. "Don't get all weepy and shit, please." He tore off sheets of paper towels and frantically offered them to Emily. "I was just giving Phil a hard time, okay? It's a brother thing. Better? Better now?"

If my life were a musical, Emily thought with satisfaction, *in this scene the role of me would be played by Judy Garland.* She imagined those big, limpid eyes, the quivering lower lip, the voice that throbbed with vulnerability. "Please, Auntie Em,"—she sobbed, deeply in character—"don't let them take Toto—"

"Awww, don't look at me that way!" Mark begged. "I'll lend you the freakin' money! Two conditions only."

"What are they?" said Philip, crossing his arms.

"One, no more crying." Mark pointed at Emily, who regained her composure instantly. "Two: you have to introduce me to *her.*" He gestured at the wall above Philip's desk.

Philip turned away, mortified, but Emily looked up to see what Mark was talking about. It was Stephanie Dawson's picture, torn out of an *Aurora* souvenir program and autographed in fat black marker.

"Stephanie!" she exclaimed.

Mark let out a low wolf whistle. "Ever since you put her picture up, the redheaded vixen has been haunting my dreams, dude."

"Why do you want to meet her?" asked Philip.

Mark rolled his eyes. "Because she's hot, that's why! Seriously, Phil, this is the kind of thing I'm talking about—"

"She probably has a boyfriend." Philip cut him off. He was not interested in hearing the rest of what Mark might have to say, especially in front of Emily.

Mark waggled his eyebrows suggestively. "All hot girls have boyfriends. You can't let that kind of thing stand in your way."

Philip stood up. Emily half expected him to refuse this outrageous demand, tell Mark to find his own dates, declare his secret love for Stephanie—something dramatic, anyway. "Fine," he said. "I'll send Ian an e-mail right now and set it up."

As Philip left the room, Emily was flooded with the most awful feeling. *All hot girls have boyfriends.* Was that true? She certainly didn't have a boyfriend. She had Philip, but that was hardly the same thing, was it?

"You know, maybe you should keep away from Stephanie," she said to Mark.

Mark chuckled and sat down on his rumpled twin bed. "Jealous, huh? Don't worry, I'll still be single when you're old enough for me. I'm not really into commitment, you know!" He giggled hilariously.

Emily willed herself not to blush. "No, the thing is, I think Philip likes her."

"Nah," Mark said. "He doesn't. He doesn't like girls."

"How do you know that?" Emily tried to hide the intensity of her curiosity.

" 'Cause if he did, why wouldn't he like you?" Mark said, leaning back on his pillows. "You're a babe. All this 'we're just friends' stuff—kinda whiffs of BS, don'tcha think?"

Thoughts of this nature had occurred to Emily before, but not in so many words.

"I'm a babe?" she asked.

"*Hella* babe." Mark nodded. "A soulful, raven-haired beauty. You call me when you're a senior, 'kay?" Mark grinned at her. He was kind of charming, if you ignored the fried brain cells and the Doritos stuck to his teeth.

"Filthy sneakers on the bed, that is so gross," Philip said, reentering the room. He pushed Mark's feet to the ground.

"Ian was online. He says Stephanie is coming to see his show at LaGuardia tomorrow afternoon. If we go, you can meet her then."

"Awesome," Mark said, grinning like a chimp. "Dude! I'm gonna go see a musical!"

17

"ANYONE CAN WHISTLE"

Anyone Can Whistle
1964. Music and lyrics by Stephen Sondheim,
book by Arthur Laurents

The Fiorello H. LaGuardia High School of Music & Art and Performing Arts was one block west of Lincoln Center, home of the Metropolitan Opera, New York City Opera, New York City Ballet, the Juilliard School—in other words, it was a neighborhood Mark didn't know very well. Much to Philip's embarrassment, Mark was gawking and pointing like a tourist.

"I totally want to meet this sexy granny of yours," Mark said as they waited for the light to change at Sixty-fifth and Amsterdam. "The story about the boyfriend going blind and the Winnebago is so bogus, it's like something out of a freakin' musical, heh heh."

Emily ignored the "sexy granny" comment; she'd never told anyone about the Victoria's Secret stash in Grandma

"Like Bernadette Peters," Stephanie added. A collective "oooh" of adoration emanated from Ian, Philip, and Emily. Stephanie waited for them to finish before she continued. "She's a goddess onstage in New York, but you hardly ever see her in a movie, or on TV. Unless it's the Tony Awards broadcast."

"But that doesn't make sense," Mark said. "It's dumb."

Ian shrugged. "It's Broadway."

When Emily excused herself to use the restroom, Stephanie followed in hot pursuit. Emily noticed that she didn't have to pee, but she did want to chat.

"You know what I am *loving* about this guy Mark?" Stephanie said as she fluffed her hair in the mirror while Emily washed her hands. "There is not one gay bone in that man's body, that's what I'm loving about Mark. What a relief! Not that I don't love Ian. I love, I love, I *adore* Ian. My best buddy. Like you and Philip!"

"Uh-huh," said Emily.

"But when you meet someone new and you make plans to get together and you think it might be a date, so you 'work your assets' a little bit"—Stephanie giggled, as if Emily would know what she meant—"it's *such* a bummer! After five minutes you're sitting there and you're thinking, whoa, I put on my push-up bra and shaved my legs and all for nothing, you know?"

"Five minutes? How can you tell?" Emily didn't own a push-up bra, but she was nevertheless intrigued by Stephanie's theory.

"Honey," laughed Stephanie. "Forget all the 'gaydar' clichés. Plenty of straight guys are fussy about their looks and go to Off-Broadway plays, and plenty of gay guys are slobs and work for the city. The difference is"—and she paused for a moment to blot her crimson lipstick—"a straight guy will be *attracted* to you. And he'll let you know."

"But what if you're not sure?" asked Emily. All she had with her was some Chapstick.

"If you're not sure," Stephanie said, "then neither is he."

It was time for Stephanie to go to the theatre. Mark was having a hard time wrapping his head around the idea that the same person he had just watched eat a baked potato and salad was now going to perform on a Broadway stage. To his horror, Philip thought he recognized the beginnings of a stage-struck gleam in his brother's eye.

"And I was really looking forward to seeing a musical today, too!" Mark said, gazing at Stephanie like a lost puppy. "Can I come see yours?"

Stephanie pouted, which was one of her more charming expressions. "Believe me, there isn't a single ticket to be had. If there were I would have gotten some for my pals, here." She threw her arm around Philip's shoulders. "But really? You like musicals? Lots of guys don't."

"Sure I do!" Mark enthused. "But no sweat about the tickets. I'll go catch a movie and take you out for a drink later, after you get off work, okay?"

Stephanie kicked Emily meaningfully under the table. *See?* her kick said, clear as a bell. *Straight guy! What'd I tell ya?*

Mark peeled off a few bills from the fat roll in his pocket and tucked them in Philip's shirt pocket. "You better get home, though, young man. School tomorrow and all that. Make sure you finish your homework." He glanced at

Stephanie, who was completely buying the caring-big-brother routine. Apparently she didn't notice Philip's gritted teeth. "If you get hungry, order yourself some pizza."

Aurora *was closing*. . . . *No tickets left* . . . *ten thousand shows could never be enough*. . . .

Seeing Stephanie head off to the Rialto Theatre for the fifth-from-last performance of Aurora—it was too much for Emily. As the eastbound train carried her and Philip homeward once more, Emily steeped uselessly in her anger, like a tea bag left in the cup long after the water has gone cold and murky.

Stephanie had Aurora, Emily fumed, her thoughts relentless as the *chug-chug* of the train. *Stephanie had a boyfriend and a date. Stephanie was an urban sophisticate who wore red lipstick and understood the male mind.* Could anxious, unadorned Emily Pearl from the suburbs ever metamorphose into such a confident and attractive creature? No. It was simply unimaginable.

Emily's gut ached and her skin felt hot. She decided she must be in mourning for *Aurora*. She'd taken Intro to Psych last semester, so she knew about the five stages of grief: denial, anger, bargaining, depression, acceptance. These were called the Kübler-Ross stages, named after the woman who identified them.

The second stage was anger. Maybe that's what Emily was feeling. At the moment, she wanted to growl at everyone she saw.

"Do you feel angry?" Emily said to Philip, somewhat out of context. But surely he was in mourning for the show as well, and would understand how she felt.

"Yeah," he said. "In fact, I'm planning to kill Mark the next time I see him. Why? Do I look angry?"

"No," said Emily. "I was just thinking about the Keebler Elves. And how one of the stages is anger, and that I've been really short-tempered lately, like I just wanted to fight with someone."

Philip frowned. "Cookies make you angry?"

"Kübler-Ross!" Emily buried her head in her hands, her dark hair falling over them like a curtain. "I hate when I do that!"

"Do what?" Philip was getting more lost by the minute. Girls could be very confusing, that was the truth. He'd been thinking about girls a bit extra lately, ever since Mark had said what he'd said to their mother. Not that Philip hadn't thought about girls before, of course he had; half the people he knew were girls, after all—

"Saying something different than what I was planning to say," explained Emily. "It's like my brain is putting words in my mouth."

"Listen, Em," Philip said. "I've been thinking, and I was wondering if you wanted to be my girlfriend."

Emily stared at him, speechless.

Obviously Emily's brain-mouth problem was contagious. Philip had not planned to say anything remotely like that. He'd been planning to ask her what she'd thought of the *Anyone Can Whistle* cast recording he'd lent her. A young Angela Lansbury and some obscure Sondheim songs; it was a particular favorite of his.

"Angela Lansbury!" he sputtered. The truth was, Mark's taunts had set him wondering—why *wasn't* Emily his girlfriend? They spent all their free time together. They had stuff in common. She didn't, as far as he knew, like anyone else. And she was a perfectly presentable person—nice-looking, intelligent, a little offbeat by most people's standards but so was Philip, and she had a good heart.

It made perfect sense, except for the fact that they'd been best friends for almost three years and the idea of romance had never even come up. Why was that?

Emily was still staring at him. "Wow," she said. "Wow. Where did— When did you— I'm not sure what to say."

Philip wasn't sure, either, so he took a pen out of his backpack and started to doodle on his arm.

"You don't have to answer," he mumbled, not able to look at her. "I don't know why I said that, I shouldn't have. Forget it, okay?"

"Okay," said Emily. Did he want her to be his girlfriend or not? And could she even picture Philip as her boyfriend? Philip was so sweet, so not like other boys—but could she imagine them holding hands, kissing, going to the prom? She could easily imagine them going to *Aurora*, but that was never going to happen again. *Never, never, never.* She felt the tears well up.

"Hey," Philip said, panicky. "Hey! Don't get upset. I'm sorry, I don't know what I was thinking. Let's not talk about it, okay, just forget what I said."

"Okay," Emily said again. She'd never been so confused, but luckily they were almost home.

18

"THE OLDEST ESTABLISHED PERMANENT FLOATING CRAP GAME IN NEW YORK"

Guys and Dolls
1950. Music and lyrics by Frank Loesser,
book by Abe Burrows and Jo Swerling

Thursday. Four performances left.

It was very late when Mark got back to D-West. Philip was already in bed, sleeping, but that didn't prevent Mark from starting a conversation the moment he entered the room.

"Stephanie Dawson, now, *that's* a woman," he said, flicking on the bedroom light. Philip groaned and pulled his pillow over his head. "Did you know she's a dancer? And what a head for business! Dude, I want in on this Lanerick Rep thing!"

Philip didn't answer, so Mark punched him in the leg. "I'm serious. I'm in for five grand. You bring the money to the guy's office tomorrow, got that? Steph told me his name. Davy Davidson, Frankie Frankenfart, some wacko name like that."

"Stevie Stephenson." Philip mumbled. "School tomorrow. Go see him yourself."

"I can't, you idiot. Look at me!" Mark shook his mane of frizzy hair. "Do I look like a man of the theatuh?"

Philip opened one bleary eye. "You look like Cheech. Or Chong. One of those guys."

"Exactly! A professional like Frankenfart wants to do business with his own kind. You're going."

"Why should I?" said Philip.

"Five thousand dollars," said Mark. "Four for me, one for you. The one is a loan. When the investment pays off you can use the profit to make good on the sexy granny loan. I'm making you an offer you can't refuse. Capish?"

Philip didn't capish, really, but he was still half asleep. He grunted and tried to hide under the covers. "You owe me money, dancing boy!" Mark yelled in his ear. "How else are you and your cute little nongirlfriend planning to pay me back?"

This was a fair question, and it was one for which Philip did not yet have an answer.

"Steph told me she always had this fantasy about having a boyfriend who's a producer, huh. How hot is that?" Mark kicked off his shoes and climbed into bed. "Did you know that Nathan Lane was the voice of the meerkat in *Lion King*? Steph told me. He's awesome."

"He's the One Sure Thing, all right," said Philip. Going to Stephenson's office would be a huge pain, but even more excruciating was listening to Mark try to dish about theatre. Philip looked at his clock radio. It was almost two a.m.

"Love that meerkat," mumbled Mark as he drifted off. "Cute as a button, man."

★　★　★

Philip didn't see Emily until study hall, when they met in the library as usual. His horrible faux pas of the previous day made him afraid Emily might want to explore this boyfriend-girlfriend concept further, or talk about "the relationship"— didn't girls always want to do that?—but he needn't have worried. Emily was so grossed out by the notion of investing Mark's money in the Lanerick Rep that that was all she wanted to discuss.

"No!" cried Emily, after Philip had explained the plan. "That would be like—something!" She struggled to remember the phrase. "Like giving comfort to the enemy! That's what Grandma Rose calls it in *Fiddler* when one of Tevye's daughters falls in love with a Russian soldier."

Philip didn't quite see the connection. He shrugged. "Everyone seems to think it's a sure thing. If we can make back the money we borrowed from Mark, wouldn't that be worth it?"

"What if the Lanerick Rep is a bust, though?" Emily asked. "Then we'd owe Mark a thousand dollars more than we do now."

It was a risk, but Philip had no idea how to calculate the odds. They needed advice, the kind of advice that could only come from a threatre-savvy person with an inside track. They might try Morris, but they didn't know how to get in touch with Morris other than to wander Times Square looking for him.

There was someone else they could ask, though. And two of the library computers were available.

AURORAROX: yoo-hoo
BwayPhil: Anybody home?

SAVEMEFROMAURORA: Phil & Roxie, where've you guys been lately?

SAVEMEFROMAURORA: I was worried, thought maybe you did something dumb out of desperation.

BwayPhil: We're okay.

AURORAROX: not really, though

SAVEMEFROMAURORA: That hothead Marlena had to go and spill the beans—did you get any tix by some miracle?

AURORAROX: no

AURORAROX: all gone by the time we got there

SAVEMEFROMAURORA: Ah, too bad. Wish I could help ya but— well, too bad.

AURORAROX: i thought you hated Aurora

SAVEMEFROMAURORA: Oh, I do, but now that it's terminal I can afford to get sentimental.

BwayPhil: Listen, we have a question for you, do you mind?

SAVEMEFROMAURORA: Depends what it is, but fire away.

BwayPhil: It's about the Lanerick Rep.

SAVEMEFROMAURORA: Can you believe that John Simon? "Like printing (expletive) money." In the Times they publish this filth!

BwayPhil: Is it, though?

SAVEMEFROMAURORA: Is it what?

BwayPhil: A surefire hit? Because a friend of ours has a small amount of money to invest and we were wondering what you thought—

SAVEMEFROMAURORA: I'm shocked, shocked! The body of Aurora is not even cold and listen to you!

AURORAROX: please

AURORAROX: "our friend" is desperate

SAVEMEFROMAURORA: I think your friend should collect baseball cards is what I think. What people pay for memorabilia, it's un- believable.

AURORAROX: hypothetically, though

AURORAROX: what would a person make?

AURORAROX: if they invested money in this Lanerick Rep

AURORAROX: and it does as well as everyone says?

SAVEMEFROMAURORA: It's all a crap game, of course. But you are relentless and pushy, Rox, and I like that, so I will answer. Hypothetically, then—I'd say a person would make ten times the money. That's conservative.

BwayPhil: Ten times? That's a 1000% return—that's crazy.

SAVEMEFROMAURORA: You know what they say, kid:

SAVEMEFROMAURORA: You can't make a living in the theatre—

SAVEMEFROMAURORA: but you can make a killing.

Philip looked at his watch. "If we leave now we can make the twelve-thirty-seven train and be at Stephenson's office by two." He looked at Emily with growing excitement. "Ten times the money, Emily. That makes one thousand into ten thousand—more than we borrowed from Mark!"

"Okay," Emily said. She wasn't sure about this, but if Philip and SAVEME thought it was the right thing to do . . .

BwayPhil: Okay, thanks, that's all we needed to know—

AURORAROX: thanks saveme!!!!!!!

"Emily Pearl! Just the person I was looking for!"

Emily whipped her head around in terror. Why would Mr. Henderson be looking for her? It could only be bad news.

"Uh, hello, Mr. Henderson," she mumbled. "What's up?"

"I have a theatrical emergency to deal with, and I need your help." He was acting smug, as usual, but also seemed genuinely nervous. "You are aware, I'm sure, that the drama club production of *Fiddler on the Roof,* of which I am the director, opens this weekend?"

Like I care, Emily thought. Philip had adroitly pulled an interactive Spanish quiz up on the screen and was conjugating away.

"The roles of Tevye's five daughters are being played by some of your classmates: Michelle, Cindy, Chantal, Lorelei, and Beth. But Lorelei twisted her ankle badly during cheerleading practice this morning." Mr. Henderson made a face. "I'm short one of Tevye's daughters."

Emily dared not imagine what he was going to suggest. "Isn't four daughters enough?" she said.

"One would think," he sighed. "But *Fiddler* requires five. Lorelei might be well enough to do the show on Saturday. She might not. We need an understudy." He extended a hand to Emily. "Congratulations, Emily. You're on!"

"Me!" cried Emily. "Why me?

"Because I figured you were the only girl in the school who knew all the music already, am I right?" Chagrined, Emily nodded. "Besides, you desperately need some extra credit."

"Do I have to?" she whimpered.

"Only if you want to pass English. Rehearsal is today after school." He smiled. "Welcome to the theatre, Emily."

" 'Welcome to the Theatre.' " Philip turned around and stared at Mr. Henderson. "*Applause,* 1970. Music by Charles Strouse, lyrics by Lee Adams, book by Betty Comden and Adolph Green. Based on the film *All About Eve.*"

"Oh, dear." Mr. Henderson seemed amused. "Not another one. Just promise me you won't pursue it professionally; it's a penniless life of heartbreak and disappointment. You know what they say: you can't make a living in the theatre—"

"But you can make a killing." Emily and Philip said it together, wide-eyed.

"Precisely. I'll see you at rehearsal, Emily."

With that, Mr. Henderson made his exit.

19

"HOW ARE THINGS IN GLOCCA MORRA?"

Finian's Rainbow
1947. Music by Burton Lane, lyrics by E. Y. Harburg,
book by E. Y. Harburg and Fred Saidy

And so, however improbably, thanks to a clumsy cheerleader, Emily spent the afternoon learning the choreography for "Matchmaker, Matchmaker" from *Fiddler*, and Philip ended up traveling to Stevie Stephenson's Manhattan office alone.

After Mr. Henderson left, Emily had sputtered and ranted about how she was now convinced Mr. Henderson was SAVE-MEFROMAURORA—her own English teacher! What were the odds? Philip thought it was probably a coincidence that Mr. Henderson had used the same expression as SAVEME, but he had a train to catch and no time to debate the issue. Impulsively, he'd leaned over and kissed Emily goodbye, on the cheek. Then he left the library without looking back, just in case she was wiping it off.

It was true Philip didn't have much in the way of sexual experience and that his best friend was a girl whom, until today, he'd never even attempted to kiss. But that didn't mean he was gay, did it, and what the hell business was it of Mark's anyway? And why did Mark have to get their mother involved? Now poor Mrs. Nebbling would devote all her legal and costume-making skills to securing Philip's right to marry another boy and designing outlandish outfits for him to wear in the Greenwich Village Halloween parade. Didn't the woman have enough to deal with? No question: Mark was dead meat.

This line of thinking kept Philip occupied during his trip on the Long Island Rail Road, his duck-and-dodge through the crowds of Penn Station to the street, his long-legged speed walk up Eighth Avenue and around the corner of Forty-fourth Street to the Sardi's building, which housed Stevie Stephenson's office. He could walk much faster when Emily wasn't trotting along next to him trying to keep up, and it felt good to exert himself.

It had been easy to find Stephenson's office address on the Internet. Philip pressed the elevator button and waited. He patted his coat pocket, which drooped with the weight of five thousand dollars in cash. An offer, certainly, that even a man of Stephenson's extravagant means couldn't refuse.

Nobody was around when Emily got home after rehearsal. It was a relief in a way, because it meant Emily didn't have to make happy chitchat about her Eleanor Roosevelt High School drama club debut. In *Fiddler*, no less! Emily had had no trouble learning the part, but it was pretty hilarious watching Mr. Henderson dance around like a starry-eyed teenage girl as he taught her the steps.

Her parents would be home soon, though. Emily wondered when Grandma Rose and Stan would make their getaway. The Winnebago had been purchased and insured, the tank filled with gas, and the rig inconspicuously parked in front of Birchwood Gardens D-West (this had been Mark's idea—you had to give him credit for knowing how to hide things in plain sight), but Grandma Rose remained mum on the timing of their departure.

"If you don't know, the Cossacks can't torture it out of you," she'd said to Emily, patting her cheek. "Not that you wouldn't try not to tell. But parents have ways. So how do you like my Stan, huh? What a cutie!"

All hot grandmas have boyfriends. Even if their granddaughters don't. Emily felt a tinge of bitterness as she grabbed a bag of Chex Party Mix and brought it with her to her room. She wasn't supposed to eat in there, but at the moment all she wanted to do was lie in bed with a forbidden snack and listen to the *Aurora* CD. She especially wanted to hear Marlena Ortiz sing the heartbreaking second-act reprise of "Never Be Enough," which always made Emily cry.

What a confusing day, she thought. *Mr. Henderson either is or isn't SAVEME and Philip either does or doesn't want to be my boyfriend and I've been kidnapped by a high school musical that opens in two days—but I might or might not be going on, depending on Lorelei's stupid ankle. . . .*

The only thing that seemed certain was that *Aurora* was closing, and Emily would never, ever see it again.

If you're going to cry anyway, better to have a sad song to do it to. Emily popped the CD in her stereo and stretched out on the bed.

Miss O'Malley's voice had a gentle Irish lilt, but she still sounded very firm on the phone.

"No, dear, I'm terribly sorry. All the house seats are spoken for. That's right, have a good day now."

"Mr. Stephenson's office—oh, hello, Mr. Mayor. I wish I could help you, love, but Stevie's already promised them all . . ."

"Hello, Stephenson Productions. Ah, Mr. Trump! The flowers you sent were too much now, darlin'. Yes, I know how you love the show, and if I had a single ticket left I'd give it to you for sure. . . ."

While she was talking, she cocked one eyebrow at Philip and gestured for him to have a seat. The reception area of Stephenson's office was clubby and rich-looking, with leather sofas and dark wood paneling. The only whiff of theatre about the place was the copy of *Variety* lying on one of the coffee tables, peeking out from underneath the day's *Wall Street Journal*.

"Dearie me! Tell the prince I'm much obliged, but I can't possibly entertain his proposal—he's got quite enough wives already. No, no house seats for him, either, so sorry, Mr. Trump. Cheers!"

She hung up the phone and turned to Philip. "Can you believe the cheek?" she said. "That lot could've bought out the whole theatre any night of the week for the past three years. Now that there's not so much as a barstool left to sell, they call looking for a handout. Even if I had a ticket I'd say no, but I don't, of course." She eyed him suspiciously. "That's not why you're here, is it, dear?"

"No! I know. It's completely sold out," Philip said quickly. This may have been the first time in his life he felt in the same boat as Donald Trump.

" 'Tis," she said, adding another packet of sugar to her tea. "Why are you here, then? Selling chocolates for school, is it?"

"I would like to speak to Mr. Stephenson," Philip said, trying to sound businesslike. "It's a financial matter."

"Aren't they all, darlin', aren't they all," she clucked, punching buttons on her phone. "Hello, Mr. Stephenson's office—ah, not you again! Now listen, you barrel of monkeys, I just turned down the crown prince of Arabia, what makes you think I'll say yes to you? Hang on, then." She pressed another button. "Mr. Stephenson, Nathan Lane is on line one." Miss O'Malley turned to Philip with a sigh. "It's the funny ones who are saddest in real life, you know."

Philip didn't know, and he was sure he didn't want to. "I have some money to invest," he said. "Will I be able to see Mr. Stephenson soon?"

"What are you, lad, fourteen? Fifteen?"

"Sixteen," said Philip.

"Stevie was twelve when he produced his first show, did you know that?" Miss O'Malley sipped her tea. "If you've got money to invest, he'll see you. Office policy. It's 'on principle,' he says, but it's more of a superstition if you ask me." She glanced at her phone. "Pardon me—when Mr. Lane's on the phone I've got orders to interrupt after two minutes, otherwise it goes on the whole blessed day."

Miss O'Malley stood, smoothed her skirt, and walked on a pair of formidably high-heeled pumps to the door of Mr. Stephenson's office. She rapped sharply, twice, and opened the door a crack.

Philip heard a muffled roar from inside Stephenson's office. Rage or laughter, he couldn't tell.

" 'Like printing [expletive] money!' Can you believe that joker! But that's you, baby, the human printing press. Hang on, Eileen is telling me something—"

"It's time to leave for your doctor's appointment, Mr. Stephenson," she shouted, too loudly.

Stephenson waved the phone in Miss O'Malley's direction before putting it back to his ear. "Hear that? Gotta run. Love you too. Now start printing!" Stephenson slammed the phone down and wiped his brow. "Comedians! They break your heart."

"There's a boy to see you," Miss O'Malley said. "With money to invest."

"A boy with money?" Stephenson smiled. "Show him in."

The CD clicked forward to track fourteen—this was it, Emily's favorite song. Emily reached for her Chex, but the bag had slid off the bed and onto the floor. It probably had spilled, which made her reluctant to look, so she didn't. She just burrowed more deeply into the pillows.

In the first act of *Aurora*, "Never Be Enough" was an upbeat song of love triumphant over all. One intermission and several broken hearts later, Aurora was a different woman. Now she knew that all her dreams wouldn't necessarily come true. Hence, the second-act reprise: a slow, sad version of the happy, peppy song everyone had liked so much in the first act.

How can ballad tempo and a minor key make the same song mean something completely different? Emily wondered. *And why do you never hear happy reprises of sad songs?*

As the music filled her room, Emily closed her eyes and had a kind of waking dream. She was onstage at the Rialto Theatre, singing her heart out, when she looked out at the audience and spotted a pale, crying teenage girl with long dark hair, clutching her program in her lap.

Poor kid, dream-Emily thought as she strode across the stage in a circle of light. This kind of light was called a follow-spot, because no matter where you went on stage, the spotlight followed you, like a bubble of love.

Poor kid. I'm gonna sing this one for her. And in her dream, Emily onstage sang her heart out for Emily in the audience, and it was happy and sad at the same time.

I'm having a dream ballet, thought Emily as she dozed off. *Just like in* Oklahoma. . . .

Philip's meeting with Stevie Stephenson only lasted a few minutes.

"In the first place," Stephenson said sternly, once Philip had managed to stammer out his offer, "five thousand dollars is not a real amount of money."

Philip was bewildered; it seemed like an enormous sum to him. "Okay," he said, sounding shaky. "How much is?"

"I don't know!" shouted Stephenson. "But I know it when I see it! And in the second place, do you honestly think I need MORE investors for the Lanerick Rep? This is a COUP! It is the INVESTMENT OPPORTUNITY OF A LIFETIME! Only a very, very select few, handpicked by ME, were PER-MITTED to put money into this project! And those people will make a FORTUNE. And they will OWE ME FOR LIFE."

In fact, it had taken all the self-discipline Stephenson pos-sessed not to put up all the money (and thus grab all the profit) himself, but he wasn't an idiot. If he shut his best investors out of this, a surefire hit, where would they and their checkbooks be when he wanted to produce his next show? One that, un-like the Lanerick Rep, had an actual chance of failure?

There could only be one Lanerick Rep in a career, Stephenson knew this. He'd peaked, and the trick would be to make it last. He harbored fantasies of Lane and Broderick growing old together, still playing at the Rialto—they could do a gay spin on *The Gin Game*, perhaps, with Broderick in the Katharine Hepburn role. Or a senior-citizen version of *The Odd Couple*—they'd call it *The Old Couple*.

The Old Couple, *ha!* That would get a laugh out of Eileen; he'd have to remember to tell her when he was done yelling at this kid with the piggy bank. Tantrums were to Stephenson what meditation was to a monk: a daily cleansing practice. He believed his temper was other people's problem; his blood pressure clocked in at an enviable 110 over 60, and he slept like a baby every night of his life.

"Does that mean you don't need any more money?" Philip asked hesitantly. Math whiz that Philip was, he was regretting not having done more research on the financial structures of theatrical producing. Clearly it was more complicated than he'd imagined.

"NO!" screamed Stephenson. He seemed to relish the volume of his own voice. "I mean, YES, I don't need any more money! Didn't you see *The Producers*? You can only sell a hundred percent of anything! And the Lanerick Rep is SOLD!"

Philip, of course, had not seen *The Producers*. But he had seen *Aurora*, a lot. And the money for all those hundreds of tickets—Grandma Rose's money, Emily's college money, her bat mitzvah money, for heaven's sake!—had been going, at least in part, into the pockets of this nutcase.

He was glad Emily hadn't come.

20

"A TRIP TO THE LIBRARY"

She Loves Me
1963. Music by Jerry Bock, lyrics by Sheldon Harnick, book by Joe Masteroff

Emily's house was still empty when she woke up.

Where was everyone? It was six-thirty; they should be sitting down to dinner by now. Emily wandered from room to room, quietly at first. Then she started calling out.

"Mom? Dad? Grandma?"

Emily's brain was still foggy from her nap, so she endured a full minute and a half of mounting anxiety before she thought of calling Mrs. Pearl's cell phone. (Mr. Pearl refused to carry one; he said they would only be truly useful once they could actually beam you up.)

As she grabbed the phone, her chest filled with dread, and the horrible lesson of *last times* came rushing back into her mind. *Maybe they're never coming back. Maybe this morning was the last time I'll ever see my family, maybe something horrible has happened, maybe maybe maybe—*

The call went through. Her mother's cell was ringing, but it was also echoing somewhere in the house. Emily listened and walked, following the sound. Up the stairs, into the bathroom—nope, back into the master bedroom—now it was very close.

On Emily's phone the ringing stopped and her mother's voice spoke, tinny and overexcited.

"Hi, it's Laurey Pearl! Please leave a message after the beep."

There. Mrs. Pearl's cell phone was lying on the carpet, next to her treadmill, which was paused but still turned on. A pair of headphones was plugged into the portable CD player Mrs. Pearl used when she did her workout (Mr. Pearl had wanted to get her an iPod for her birthday, but Mrs. Pearl pooh-poohed it as an extravagance. What would they think, should they ever find out, of the small fortune Emily had spent on theatre tickets? Emily couldn't bear to imagine.)

A low, insect-like hum was coming out of the headphones. Emily picked them up and listened—

> *I believe in you!*
> *I believe in you!*

It was Matthew Broderick, in *How to Succeed*.

Emily turned off the treadmill. Something was horribly, horribly wrong.

The thought of a crud like Stephenson spending Emily's money on monogrammed shirts and lunches at Sardi's was making Philip really angry.

Not blind, storming-around angry—if he'd been that kind of angry, Philip never would have noticed the file folder marked "Final Box Office Statements" lying on Miss O'Malley's desk when Stephenson finally threw him out of the office ("Now go home and join the DRAMA CLUB!" were Stephenson's parting, apoplectic words).

No, this was the kind of deep, righteous anger that was the prerequisite for superhero powers. It gave you laser-sharp vision and ninja invisibility; it made you deft of hand and fleet of foot, not to mention somewhat unscrupulous.

Miss O'Malley was at the hot water dispenser making herself a fresh cup of tea. Her desk had plenty of paper on it; if some disappeared it would not immediately be apparent. Certainly Philip would have enough time to get downstairs to the street and disappear into the throngs of tourists and playgoers, hucksters and working folk. For a boy on the lam, Times Square was one big human shield.

How convenient, Philip thought as he slid the file folder into his backpack. *I've been meaning to close out my* Aurora *spreadsheets. These will save me a lot of time.*

He whistled as he rode down in the elevator, even though there were other people riding with him. Philip was so pleased with himself he decided to drop by the Drama Book Shop. Only a few blocks away, this was a whole store stocked only with books about the theatre. Philip sometimes browsed there but never bought anything because of his perpetual lack of funds.

Now, though, Philip had a pocketful of money, and what he wanted was information. The Drama Book Shop was the place to go, definitely. But he hardly expected to run into someone he knew in the producing section.

The absurd thing was, he didn't even notice her standing

there, reading glasses perched on the end of her gorgeous nose, with her head buried in a book called *Going Platinum! The A–Z Guide to Producing Your Hit Record*.

No, Marlena Ortiz was the one who recognized *him*.

"Well, hello there!" she said, peering over her glasses. "The boy from the stage door, right? Number one fan? With the Sharpie?" She mimed signing her name. The book Philip was looking at slipped out of his hands and thudded to the floor.

"Oh—oh my God," he stammered. "Marlena. Miss Ortiz, I mean. What are you doing here?"

"Actors read books." She smiled her killer smile. "Don't tell."

"I won't," Philip said, while thinking, *I am such an idiot.* She was so pretty close up, in the daylight. None of that heavy stage makeup he was used to seeing her in, no fuzzy mittens or striped legwarmers or floppy velvet hats—just black leggings tucked into pointed-toe boots, a faded denim shirt, and a thin silk scarf tied loosely around her neck. She looked almost like an ordinary human being, only much, much more fabulous.

"But what are you doing here, *numero uno?*" she asked. "In the producing section? I would have thought you'd be over by the audition monologues. You could be an actor. You're so handsome."

Philip felt his face getting hot. "Not me!" he said. "I'm more—of a numbers guy, I guess."

"That's good," she said, suddenly quite serious. "Trusting other people to manage your business is a terrible mistake. That's a lesson I already learned." She gestured with the book in her hand and laughed, as if to say: *How ironic, that a great talent like me should have to learn about subsidiary rights and direct mail campaigns!*

"I know what you mean." *Ugh*. Philip's attempts at banter were making him feel like the biggest flop on Broadway.

"Show business needs people like you." Marlena's lower lip quivered with feeling. "With a head for money"—she tapped Philip's forehead with her fingertip—"and a heart of gold." She laid her hand on Philip's chest and spoke dramatically to her own thumb. "A heart that loves the theatre."

The heat of Marlena's hand cut right through three layers of clothing and settled on his skin. Philip wanted to close his eyes and stand there forever, soaking up Marlena's warmth, but he was too flustered to let the moment last. "How's the show?" he said, feeling like a fool. "How's it going?"

"It's the same every night." Marlena took her hand away and ran it through her hair. "You haven't been around lately, huh?"

"We couldn't get any tickets. We tried," Philip added, looking down in shame.

"Wait," Marlena said. She reached into her purse. What she pulled out made Philip's heart race.

"Two tickets for tomorrow night." Marlena held them up right in front of his face. "If I offered them to you, would you want them?"

Oh my God, thought Philip. "Oh my God," he said. "Yes!"

Marlena looked at him with eyes like melting chocolate. "And if I only had one?"

But there were two tickets right there, in her hand. "Yes," he said. That had to be the right answer. "I would take one."

"What about your friend?" Marlena asked. "The girl with the dark hair?"

Apparently this was some kind of game, but Philip had no idea how to play. "Emily," he said, stalling. "Her name is Emily."

"I think Emily loves you." Marlena splayed the tickets like a winning hand at poker. "I see it in her face when the dancers flirt with you at the stage door. Especially that little one, Stephanie. She's kind of a tart."

"That's why I would want the ticket," Philip said. He felt like he was hearing his own voice from a distance. "For Emily."

Marlena's eyes started to glisten. She pulled one ticket from the pair.

"Here. My gift to you is to let you give this gift to her," she said. "Perform an act of love, in real life. It will make you much happier than any show ever could. Even a show that stars *me*!" Marlena laughed.

"Oh my God," said Philip. *Would it have been so awful for her to give me both of the tickets?* "Thank you!"

She looked at her watch. "Almost seven. I have to get to the theatre. Tell your friend she'll be sitting with the head of RCA." Marlena quickly stashed the other ticket and snapped her purse shut. "Hey, don't forget your book."

Philip picked it up off the floor with sweaty hands. *How To Produce a Broadway Musical.* "Got it, thanks," he said.

Marlena glanced at his book, and smiled again. "Looks like I'll be working for you someday," she purred. *"Adios, numero uno."*

To: AURORAROX
Subject: A Present for You
Em,

I have a present for you.
Can't say what.
But you can pick it up tomorrow night.

At eight o'clock.

At the Rialto Theatre.

Philip

Philip pressed Send and took his hands off the keyboard. To think the first great act of love he'd performed in sixteen years on the planet was executed under the fluorescent lights of a Kinko's in Midtown. They charged by the minute for Internet computers, so he'd kept it short.

Would this "act of love" make him as happy as Marlena seemed to think it would? Did Emily love him? Did he love her? It was so hard to know these things. But an act of love, delivered from a safe distance by e-mail—you couldn't go wrong with that.

For the rest of the evening, during the train ride back to Rockville Centre and the fast walk through dark streets to Birchwood Gardens, Philip kept imagining the look on Emily's face when she got the message.

"What's going on?" cried Emily. "What happened? Where were you? Where is Grandma?" Emily had been watching a rerun of the *Making of* Annie documentary on PBS and was just about to go check her e-mail when her parents finally walked in. Her father was still dressed for work and her mother wore a tracksuit, but they had perfectly matched dour expressions on their faces.

"Emily! Calm down," said her mother firmly. "Grandma is in the hospital, but it's nothing serious. You can see her tomorrow."

"I'm going to make coffee," said Mr. Pearl, marching

grimly off to the kitchen. Mr. Pearl never drank coffee after dinner.

"The hospital? What happened?" Emily asked, growing more upset. "Why didn't you call me? I've been going crazy here, waiting for you. I almost called the police."

Mr. Pearl appeared in the kitchen doorway, holding the empty coffeepot. "The police?" he said. "Brilliant idea! Then your grandmother would have been busted that much sooner."

"Busted?" Emily said, in a tiny voice.

Mr. Pearl stormed back into the kitchen, cursing and clattering silverware. Mrs. Pearl turned to Emily and took a deep breath.

"Emily, early this afternoon a New Jersey state trooper picked up your grandmother at a truck stop on the New Jersey Turnpike. She was driving a, one of those, what do you call them—"

"A Winnebago!" yelled Mr. Pearl from the kitchen. "And she wasn't driving! Her blind boyfriend was driving!"

Emily's heart began to sink. "Stan was driving the Winnebago?"

"Yes," said Mrs. Pearl. "He drove it right into a parked tractor trailer. And the trooper came over to see what was wrong. And—well, they gave him a hard time, apparently."

"They tried to flee!" cried Mr. Pearl, fuming. "My crazy mother and her boyfriend in a high-speed chase on the New Jersey Turnpike! In a damn Winnebago!"

"Don't exaggerate, dear. They never made it out of the parking lot." Emily could see that her mother was struggling to remain calm. "But they both got arrested, and then they took Grandma Rose to the ER because she was having trouble breathing."

"Grandma called the police officer a Cossack," added Mr. Pearl.

"Whoa," said Emily. "Wow." *Somehow this is going to end up being about me,* she thought. *I can feel it coming. . . .*

"Stan was carrying a fake ID," Mr. Pearl said ominously. "He's not supposed to drive because of his vision, but he had a counterfeit license on him. Any idea where he might have gotten that?"

"A fake ID!" exclaimed Emily. "No, not really, no."

"Emily," said Mrs. Pearl, in an equally dire tone of voice. "When we got the call from the hospital, they told us to bring all of Grandma's prescription medication. I had to go through her dresser drawers looking for the bottles."

Uh-oh, thought Emily. *Is that what this is about? Surely they don't think all those black lace nighties belong to me?*

Mr. Pearl had tossed his overcoat across the back of the sofa when he'd come in. Now he walked over to it, reached for the inside chest pocket, and took out a piece of paper.

"Emily," he repeated, as if there remained any doubt about who was the real criminal in the family. "Your mother found this with Grandma Rose's, uh, things. It's a note from you." He held the note out to her, but of course she knew what it said. "Something about a loan, and your college fund?"

21

"CLIMB EVERY MOUNTAIN"

The Sound of Music
**1959. Music by Richard Rodgers,
lyrics by Oscar Hammerstein II,
book by Howard Lindsay and Russel Crouse**

The interrogation had been pointed and businesslike, with both Mr. and Mrs. Pearl maintaining the most terrifying poker faces throughout.

In contrast, Emily's confession was teary and nearly incoherent with remorse, but only semitruthful. She explained about the *Aurora* tickets and about the money she'd borrowed from Grandma Rose to pay for them. She came clean about all the lies she'd told about where she spent her Saturday afternoons. Then she stopped.

"That's it?" said Mr. Pearl.

Emily shrugged.

"We'd hoped you might know where Stan got hold of the fake ID," said Mrs. Pearl. "Grandma was a little vague about that."

It was Emily's opinion that Mark and Stan must have struck a deal while Stan was over at Birchwood Gardens preparing the Winnebago. However, thanks to Mr. Henderson's obsession with the persuasive essay, Emily knew the difference between opinion and proof. Without proof, she thought it best to say nothing. Getting Mark in trouble would undoubtedly lead to getting Philip in trouble, and she was not going to let that happen.

"Mmmmph." She yawned. "Tired. I have a math test tomorrow."

Her parents took the hint. The trial was far from over, but the verdict had already been decided. Emily was ultragrounded—there would be no nonemergency phone use, no computer except for homework, no outings except for school, no unescorted trips to the bathroom, if Mr. Pearl had his way.

Emily was sent her to her room, to bed, but she knew from the murmuring and occasional footsteps downstairs that Mr. and Mrs. Pearl stayed up talking for a long, long time.

When Philip got back to D-West, his mother was home but asleep, and Mark was out. He put the five thousand dollars in cash under Mark's pillow, clipped together with a note: "Frankie Frankenfart says to join the drama club. Have you considered investing in a mutual fund?"

Then he checked his e-mail. He and Emily both used AOL e-mail addresses, precisely because it made it possible for each of them to see when the other had read the e-mails they exchanged. He checked the status of the note he'd sent to Emily from Kinko's.

Unread.

Huh. Odd. She always checks e-mail before going to bed.

It was too late to call, but it didn't matter. He'd see her at school in the morning. There was something fated-feeling about his inability to avoid telling her about the *Aurora* ticket in person. Maybe he was meant to witness the look on her face when he handed her the ticket. Maybe he was meant to receive, with open arms, whatever outpouring of gratitude and emotion overcame her when she found out what he'd done.

Maybe it will be such an overwhelming moment we'll forget we're just friends and kiss each other on the lips, he thought. *I wonder what that would be like.*

Friday morning. Three performances left.

"I know Grandma Rose is somewhat at fault here. She encouraged you. But that does not make what you did acceptable." Mr. Pearl was driving the way people do when they're angry—too fast in the turns, too heavy on the brake, too speedy with the gas. "You're still responsible for your own actions. Understood?"

"Yes," said Emily, slouched in the backseat. She fingered her seat belt to make sure it was still buckled. Math test be damned: her parents had both called in sick and Emily was being kept out of school to visit her grandmother in the hospital. The Pearls were not quite ready to let their wayward, fib-prone daughter out of their sight.

They all lurched sideways as Mr. Pearl palmed the wheel and skidded around the curved hospital driveway to the main entrance. The irony of Grandma Rose's being admitted to St. Francis's Catholic Hospital of Perpetual Mercy was something Emily's parents would normally joke about, if this were a joking time.

"Is Grandma coming home today?" Emily asked as she and her mother got out of the car.

"That depends," said Mrs. Pearl curtly. "Come with me, please, Emily. Your father is going to go park. Stuart, don't forget to pick up a visitor's pass at the front desk."

It wasn't until the two of them were riding up in the elevator that Mrs. Pearl spoke again.

"So all those Saturdays—the test prep, the babysitting, the laser tag birthday parties, the volunteer work at the soup kitchen—you were at the show? All those times?"

"Not all of them." Emily was getting tired of explaining this. "Most of them, though. I did play laser tag once."

She waited for some sort of explosion, but Mrs. Pearl just nodded. "I had a feeling something was up," her mother said quietly. "But I thought it was something else. I thought you might be"—there was a little pause as Mrs. Pearl searched for the right euphemism—"*involved* with that boy. Philip."

"Oh my God!" Emily almost started to laugh. "Is that why you bought me all those books?" Mrs Pearl was a great one for leaving books with titles like *Young Woman's Body: An Operational Guide* around where Emily could find them.

Mrs. Pearl looked embarrassed. "Yes, in fact."

"You must be kind of relieved, then," Emily said.

The elevator doors opened, and Emily could swear she saw her mother trying not to smile. "That still doesn't make it okay, Emily."

BwayPhil: hey!
BwayPhil: halllooooo
BwayPhil: Em, if you're out there speak up.
BwayPhil: How come you're not in school today?
BwayPhil: Are you sick?
BwayPhil: Did you get my e-mail? About the "present"?

BwayPhil: Okay, gotta run,
BwayPhil: Guess I'll call you later☹

Emily and her mother had barely set foot on the cardiac floor when they heard the PA system crackling.

"Laurey Pearl, please go to the nurses' station. Mrs. Laurey Pearl, there is a call for you at the nurses' station."

Mrs. Pearl almost knocked down an old man taking a shuffling walk with his IV stand as she sprinted to the central desk, with Emily chasing along behind. "I'm Laurey Pearl!" she yelled, like a character in a medical drama on TV. "What's the matter? What's wrong?"

The nurse looked down at a slip of paper by her phone. "I have a message here. It seems your husband got into a fender-bender in the parking lot. Would you mind going downstairs? He doesn't seem to be handling it too well."

Mrs. Pearl covered her mouth with her hand for a moment before she spoke; this was one of her signature I-must-calm-down gestures.

"Emily," she said, her voice robotically steady. "You go see Grandma. I'll take care of Daddy."

Emily watched her mother sprint back to the elevator. She fervently hoped Grandma Rose was wearing a hospital night-gown and not something from her collection of lingerie. It was too early in the day to cope with that.

"What do you mean, why didn't I throw away the note?"

Grandma Rose was sitting up in bed, in a modest flannel gown from the hospital gift shop, wearing lipstick and playing solitaire on her meal tray. She seemed offended by Emily's question. "But darling! I have every card you ever gave me!

Every birthday, every Hanukkah, every little crayon stick-figure drawing that hung on the refrigerator when you were in preschool! You think I'd throw away such a nice note?"

Grandma Rose was fine. She seemed pretty cheerful, in fact. Emily knew that Grandma Rose and her friends often worried about having to go into the hospital for one malady or other; now that she was already here, it was probably a big weight off her mind.

Emily sighed. "How's Stan?"

"I guess I shouldn't have let him drive," Grandma Rose said sheepishly. "But you should have seen the looks on his kids' faces when they got to the police station! I wish I could have stayed, but I was having a little trouble." She pointed to her chest. "Did you notice all the nuns here?" Grandma Rose added, in a loud stage whisper. "They're very nice, I have to say. But every time I see one I want to sing. 'Climb ev'ry mountain!'" She warbled it in her fragile soprano. "*The Sound of Music*. That's a good show, you know why?"

"Julie Andrews?" Emily ventured.

"You should have seen Mary Martin! But I'll tell you why." Grandma Rose gestured and knocked her meal tray askew, scattering the cards. "Because they weren't even Jewish and the Nazis came for them anyway. You see? Everybody's got problems."

"Just like in *Fiddler*, when the Cossacks come to Tevye's village," said Emily, trying to put the cards back the way they had been. "But they're only musicals, Grandma. They sing a song and they get away and everything's fine." *If only my life were like that*, Emily thought. *If only*. "Guess what?" she added. "They're doing *Fiddler* at my school. I'm one of the understudies."

"For which part?" said Grandma, suddenly interested.

"Hodel. But the girl who got cast twisted her ankle, so I'll probably be doing it."

"No, you won't." Grandma Rose closed her eyes. "Not if she's a pro. Unless she's in a coma, the show must go on."

"She's not a pro, Grandma. She's a cheerleader. It's high school. It's the drama club." Grandma Rose didn't answer, and Emily thought she might have fallen asleep.

"Zero Mostel," Grandma Rose murmured at last. "Now, *that* was a Tevye. Never again, though. No one will see Mostel's Tevye, ever, ever again. . . ." Her eyes flew open and she looked hard at Emily. "But I saw it!" she said. "Dozens of times, I saw it! And I will never forget it. It lives forever—in here." Grandma Rose tapped her forehead.

But how can you bear it when it's over? That was the question Emily desperately wanted to ask. Before she could say anything her cell phone rang—

> *Never be enough,*
> *My love for you could never be enough*

Philip! For her birthday Philip had hacked the first four bars of "Never Be Enough" into a ring tone for her, and now it was his special ring.

Her parents had been clear: she was not allowed to use the phone unless it was an emergency. A life-threatening, 911 kind of emergency.

She glanced quickly at the "No Cell Phone Use in Hospital" sign and flipped open her phone.

"Hi," she said. "I can't talk now."

"Hey," said Philip. He was nervous—imagine, being

nervous talking to Emily. "You know how hard it is to find a pay phone these days?"

"I'm not supposed to use my cell," she said, trying to keep her voice down so as not to attract the attention of the nurses.

"Go ahead and talk on your phone, darling, I'll just take a nap!" Grandma Rose called out. There was a loud whirr as she lowered the bed into a lying-down position.

"Mr. Henderson's been looking for you, he wants to know if you'll be at rehearsal later—what's that noise?" Philip asked. "Are you at the airport?"

"I'm at the hospital," said Emily.

"The hospital!" Was that why he hadn't heard from her about the ticket? "What happened? Are you okay?"

"I'm fine," said Emily. She glanced back at Grandma Rose, who had closed her eyes. "How are you?"

"I don't know. Fine, I guess." Philip's head was starting to hurt. "I sent you kind of an important e-mail but it sounds like you didn't get it yet."

"No." Emily remembered the draconian terms of her punishment and sighed. "And I might not be able to for a while. Philip, listen—a lot of stuff has happened—"

Philip hated to interrupt, but time was of the essence. "For me, too. Em, I have a present for you, but I need to give it to you right away. Can I come by your house later?"

"No!" Emily cried. "Please, *do not* come to my house." No way could she let her parents talk to Philip until she'd had a chance to coach him on his alibi. A fake student ID was one thing, a fake driver's license was entirely another—what had she been thinking, letting Philip get Mark involved?

Emily lowered her voice to a tiny whisper. "Grandma and

Stan got arrested," she breathed into the phone. "My parents found out about us borrowing the money."

"What? I can't hear you. Emily, listen," Philip said. "I wanted this to be a surprise but it sounds like I better just tell you. You won't believe this! Yesterday, at the Drama Book Shop—"

"There is absolutely no cell phone use inside the hospital, miss!" The nurse looked like she was about to bite. "It interferes with the cardiac equipment. There are signs everywhere, didn't you notice?"

Emily put up both her hands, the way caught criminals do to show they're not carrying any weapons. "I have to hang up, bye," she said quickly, in the direction of the phone, without taking her eyes off the nurse. She prayed Philip could hear her.

The nurse snatched the phone and shut it off. "I'll hold that at the nurses' station until your parents get here," she said. As she walked away, her white shoes squeaked on the linoleum. *Squeak, squeak, squeak, squeak,* fading away as she turned the corner.

If my life were a musical, thought Emily, *that wouldn't be the beginning of a song at all. Just the stupid squeaky sound of a nurse's shoes as she walks away with my cell phone.*

22

"WHO AM I?"

Les Misérables
**1987. Music by Claude-Michel Schönberg,
French lyrics by Alain Boublil,
English lyrics by Herbert Kretzmer,
book by Alain Boublil**

The humiliation! Philip had offered up his first great act of love, or tried to, and Emily had basically hung up on him.

Did she hate him now? Had he ruined their friendship for good? And—insane problem to have!—what should he do with this single, priceless, impossible-to-get ticket for tonight's third-to-last performance of *Aurora*?

After he got off the phone with Emily he'd skipped the rest of school and taken a walk, up and down all the streets of Rockville Centre, until he got too cold and came home. It was after six o'clock. He had to decide.

Should he use the ticket himself? It was tempting. He missed the show dreadfully. It would be so wonderful to sit there, nestled in the comfort of a red velvet seat, safe in the dark as the familiar music played.

Unfortunately, during at least two numbers in *Aurora* the houselights came up to half and the cast interacted directly with the audience, so Marlena would be bound to see him sitting there. Eighth-row orchestra, right next to the head of RCA.

She'd think he'd lied about Emily just to con the ticket out of her. Would she stop the show and berate him for his deceit? She'd often interrupted the opening number to yell at late-comers; Marlena was unpredictable that way. Better she see the seat empty than him sitting there.

But come on. To not use the ticket? That would be unbearable.

He took out the ticket and looked at it.

"What's that?" said Mark, yanking off his headphones. Ever since he'd started dating Stephanie, Mark had been spending less time in front of the PlayStation and more time lying in bed listening to Philip's cast albums. At the moment he was hooked on *Les Misérables*, which he couldn't remember how to pronounce no matter how many times Philip told him.

"A ticket," Philip mumbled.

"Lemme see that," said Mark, jumping up and snatching the ticket out of Philip's hands. "Dude, this is for *Aurora*! I thought these were impossible to get. *Aurora, Aurora!*" He sang and pranced around Philip. "Can I come? Seeing Stephanie on stage, that would turn me on *so* much!"

Philip couldn't believe his brother would carry on like this with their mother typing up her depositions in the next room. "There's only one," he said, grabbing the ticket back. "It's Emily's, anyway. I gave it to her. I'm just not sure she can use it."

"Awesome!" Mark punched him on the arm. "You gave it to the soulful vixen! You're gonna get some lovin' tonight. If you want it, that is!"

"No," Philip said. "We're just friends." But even he knew how lame that sounded.

"Whoa, dude." Mark looked at him in disbelief. "You gave a ticket to a sold-out Broadway show to a chick, not so you could make the ultimate moves on her, but because you're 'friends'? You gave it to her out of 'friendship'?"

"Yes."

"Whoa," Mark said. "*Whoa*. That is some gay thing to do."

"What's going on in here?" Mrs. Nebbling peeked into their bedroom. Boys' bedrooms tended to be funky, and the Nebbling boys' room was no exception. Between the gym shoes, the dirty laundry, and the half-eaten snacks that had fallen behind the bookshelves, Mrs. Nebbling would have been wise to don her hazmat suit before entering.

"How does pizza for dinner sound?" Mrs. Nebbling asked. "I've got a ton more work to do, so I'm not going to get around to making anything. Unless you boys want to cook?"

Naturally, Mrs. Nebbling thought the boys could cook. Why shouldn't she? Every time she'd called from Wilmington and asked Mark what they'd had for dinner, he'd made something up. Baked ziti. Steaks. Fried chicken. Sometimes he even mentioned a vegetable.

"Philip will make something," Mark volunteered. "You people are so good in the kitchen."

Mrs. Nebbling frowned. "Mark, come on. That's a stereotype. It's up to Philip to decide whether or not he likes to cook, or be an astronaut, or, I don't know, run for Congress—"

"Or just go see lots of Broadway musicals!" crowed Mark.

"Well, we already know he likes to do that." Mrs. Nebbling smiled. "Mushrooms, pepperoni? What'll it be?"

It's up to Philip to decide. The phrase tightened around Philip's throat. When had it ever been up to Philip to decide anything? His mother, his father, Mark—they all came and went as they pleased and did whatever they wanted, didn't they? Philip was the one who was trapped in the chaos they left behind.

He stood up, in a sudden fury. "I am not eating pizza for dinner tonight or ever again," he said. "I've eaten pizza for breakfast, lunch, and dinner four days a week for months, and that is enough for one lifetime!"

"What are you talking about, dude?" said Mark. "What about that nice steak I made you the other day? With the, what-do-you call-'ems? Carrots?"

Philip yanked open his dresser drawer and rummaged wildly for the fake ID Mark had given him for his birthday. "Steak?" he snarled. "Don't you mean 'fake'?" His intention was to shove it in his mother's face and show her just what kind of liar Mark was, but she was looking at him with such kindness he froze.

"Philip!" Mrs. Nebbling said. "Please! I know this is a stressful time for you. I've been reading about how difficult it can be for a boy your age to accept his sexual orientation, even with a supportive family structure—"

"Did you check out that PFLAG reading list I e-mailed you, Mom?" said Mark, all but batting his eyes in innocence.

"Parents, Families and Friends of Lesbians and Gays, yes, that was very thoughtful, Mark. See, Philip? There's no need to lash out at your brother and me—"

"Would you please *listen!*" said Philip, still clutching the ID in his hand. "I am not *talking* about my sexual orientation! I am talking about what I want for *dinner!* And it is not pizza. It can be hamburgers, Chinese food, cheese and crackers, or a bowl of Campbell's tomato soup, but *not pizza!* Okay?"

"Okay," said Mrs. Nebbling cautiously. "But don't you think all this anger is really about the fact that you're still struggling—"

"And stop with the gay thing!" Philip yelled. "Like whether or not I'm gay is the most important thing about me! It's not, okay? I'm sixteen years old and I've never even *had* sex with anyone, so *who cares?*"

A red-letter day this was turning out to be, but Philip was helpless to stop himself. "You're my *mother!*" he babbled on, like it needed saying. "You're the only parent I've got who lives on the same *coast* as me! Wouldn't it be more important to know if I've done my homework?" He looked at Mark, who was engrossed in pulling loose threads out of his socks. "Or if I need a ride home from school? Or who my friends are, or where I spend my time when I'm not here?"

Philip realized with horror that there were tears running down his cheeks, but it was too late to turn back. "Or if I'm happy?" he shouted. "Or what I want to be when I grow up? Or whether . . . I even . . . care . . ."

He couldn't say any more. He grabbed his backpack and bolted out of the room.

"Phil," cried Mrs. Nebbling. "Where are you going?"

"*Aurora Aurora Aurora,*" Philip answered, but it just sounded like sobbing, even to him. He didn't bother to get his coat—he just needed to leave, now.

"Come back, dude!" yelled Mark as the front door to D-West slammed shut. "You're gonna miss the pizza!"

This was how it began, and this was how it would end: Philip Nebbling, angry and on the run from what was left of his family, drowning his sorrows in the glossy, make-believe world of Broadway. *Aurora* was an urban story with a fair amount of grit, but even so, when the mean streets of the city are filled with dance numbers, and Aurora's dying mother can belt a B-natural fortissimo and hold it for sixteen beats until the audience leaps to its feet in appreciation, how bad can things really be?

Philip knew the train schedule like the back of his hand, and the 7:03 was what he needed. It was the last train out of Rockville Centre that would get you into the city in time to make curtain. *Seven-oh-three, seven-oh-three, seven-oh-three—* the chant played in his head like the rumble of train wheels as he walked, even faster than usual to keep warm.

He had no idea what time it was now, but Philip had never missed a train in his life. He was worried that his mother would guess where he was going, though, so he took the back roads and stayed off the most direct routes to the station. She was probably driving up and down those streets right now, looking for him. At least, Philip kind of hoped she was.

Perhaps that was why, when the high, hollow whistle of the train approaching the station shrieked through the cold night air, Philip was still three blocks away.

Like a thoroughbred trained to charge full tilt from the gate at the starter's pistol, at the sound of the whistle Philip started running as fast as he could, even as his brain realized there was no way, no possible way, he could ever make this train.

"Yes, Mr. Henderson, I understand. No, she's not sick, but her grandmother is in the hospital and we've had some disciplinary issues lately, so her father and I are trying to curtail any unsupervised . . . But *you* will be supervising? I see. Sprained her ankle! That's too bad. No, Emily didn't tell us. And when does the show open? . . . Tomorrow! No, she never mentioned the extra credit. I agree, grades are so important in sophomore year, the colleges certainly do pay attention. . . ."

Mrs. Pearl shut her cell phone. "Stuart, we need to drop Emily at school."

"I thought we were going to the Toyota dealership." Mr. Pearl was in a sour mood. Grandma Rose was spending one more night in the hospital—for observation, they'd said, but Mr. Pearl was convinced it was because the doctor was too busy playing golf to come by and sign her discharge papers. And the car was now in need of a new headlight.

"We have to drop Emily first. She was supposed to be at rehearsal a half hour ago." Mrs. Pearl craned her head around to the backseat. "Emily, why didn't you tell us you were in the drama club show?"

"I'm not. I'm just the understudy," Emily said. She was angry because Mr. Pearl had threatened to confiscate her phone permanently when the nurse told him what happened, though he didn't actually do it. "Why do I have to go? I thought I was grounded."

"If she doesn't want to do it, I'm all for it," said Mr. Pearl. He changed lanes and headed for the exit that would bring them to Emily's school.

"Mr. Henderson said he really, really needs your participation," Mrs. Pearl said, trying to make peace. "He said he admired your moxie for jumping in at the last minute."

"I'm not in the mood to be in a musical right now," Emily grumbled, but inside she was thinking, *Moxie? Roxie? Is this guy SAVEME or not? Why, oh why can't I talk to Philip?*

"Emily," Mrs. Pearl said sternly. "The show must go on."

23

"IT'S A HELLUVA FIX WE'RE IN"

Inferno! The Musical
Unproduced. Author unknown.

Aurora Aurora Aurora. Aurora Aurora Aurora.

Philip sat on the curb hugging his knees, with his backpack in front of his face so no one could see the grief that was written there. Hardly anyone was out anyway; the weather was getting worse and the residents of Rockville Centre were safe inside their cars, not walking about in the open air the way Philip always did.

He was shivering. He opened his backpack in the hope that there might be something stuffed in the bottom, a dirty gym shirt or hoodie that he could put on. But all Philip saw was the producing book he'd picked up yesterday at the Drama Book Shop, and the file folder he'd nicked from Miss O'Malley's desk. The excitement of meeting Marlena and being given the ticket had made him forget all about the stolen folder.

It's not so bad, he told himself as he rocked back and forth in the embrace of his own thin arms. *It's not so bad.* He had something to read. He had numbers to crunch. He needed to go somplace warm, where he could sit and be welcome and not feel like a freak.

He could only think of one place like that.

By the time Philip boarded the 7:53 in Rockville Centre and rode it all the way to Penn Station, he'd skimmed through most of the book about producing.

The concepts were straightforward enough: you raised money from investors, you used the money to put on the show, you sold tickets, and with that money you covered the "nut" and eventually paid back the investors—but if the show closed before you "recouped" (that was what they called it when you'd made back all the initial cost of the show and actually started seeing a profit), the investors kissed their money good-bye and wrote it off on their taxes as a loss.

And yet it was a puzzling endeavor. To Philip it seemed neither business nor charity, more like flushing your money down the toilet. Still, there was no shortage of people willing to put their cash into such a dicey venture.

Philip had been most surprised to learn it was standard for the writers of a musical to get six percent of the box office. Six percent! That wasn't very much, considering there would be no show at all without the writers. It seemed even skimpier when you broke it down: two percent for the book writer, two for the lyricist, and two for the composer.

Puzzling or not, these numbers calmed Philip a great deal.

He hardly noticed the moment during his train ride when eight o'clock p.m. came and went and the *Aurora* ticket in his pocket officially became garbage. It was almost nine by the time he got to Don't Tell Mama.

"Look who's here! From the hinterlands of suburbia to a piano bar near you!" Ian was leaning against the bar, a Coke in his hand. He'd had a haircut and had let a bit of stubble grow on his face since Wednesday, when Philip had seen him last. He looked more grown-up somehow, and Philip was intensely glad to see him.

"Hey," said Philip. "Looks like I came to the right place."

"It's the only place," Ian agreed. "Friendly faces and musical theatre! Where's Emily?"

"I don't know," said Philip truthfully. "I came into the city by myself."

"Huh," said Ian. "That's a first. Well, I'm pleasantly surprised to see you. Pull up a drink and have a chair. Stay close to the piano, though—I'll be performing in a bit!"

What would it be like, thought Philip as he walked across the warm, softly lit room and took a seat at Ian's table, *to sing a song or two myself?*

Chinese food for dinner on Friday nights was a Pearl family tradition, but everything seemed like a tradition to Emily at the moment. *Tradition, tradition;* after three hours of rehearsing *Fiddler* the word was stuck in her head like gum to the bottom of a chair.

That afternoon the other cast members had been there. It wasn't so bad, really. Michelle, Cindy, Chantal, and Beth gave her welcoming hugs and helped remind her which scene came next. Lorelei, who watched from the audience with her ankle in a cast and crutches propped nearby, even faked a grateful smile. "Thank you so much, Emily!" she'd said. "You saved the show!" But Emily had seen Lorelei's lips moving through the whole rehearsal, mouthing every word.

Mr. Henderson had seemed pretty tense, but whether it was because his production of *Fiddler* was opening the next day or because he was worried about concealing his secret SAVEME identity from Emily, she had no way of knowing.

Emily thought of all this as she picked at her General Tso's chicken. The vegetable egg foo yong that Grandma Rose always craved was still in its white cardboard container, unopened, since Grandma Rose wouldn't be home until tomorrow morning and nobody had thought to change the order.

Mr. Pearl was gnawing on a spare rib when the phone rang. Mrs. Pearl got up from her meal to answer, worried that it might be the hospital, but it was Stan's son. Their conversation contained a number of phrases that, to Emily's knowledge, had never been spoken in the Pearls' home before:

"Yes, of course, resisting arrest is quite serious. . . .

"It *is* a first offense, and at their age . . .

"I know, it's unfortunate that she closed the window on the officer's arm. At least he wasn't injured. . . ."

The more she talked, the more ferociously Mr. Pearl bit into the bone. "Damn!" he suddenly exclaimed, sticking a finger into his mouth. "I think I lost a filling."

"I have to go," said Mrs. Pearl, on the phone. "But we'll see you tomorrow, at the lawyer's office. Yes, good night!"

She sat down just as Mr. Pearl got up to go examine his tooth. "Tell her about tomorrow," he mumbled, exploring his mouth with his finger and peering into the hall mirror.

"What's tomorrow?" Emily knew that whatever her parents

had cooked up for tomorrow had to be bad, but she didn't care. Every conceivable torment paled beside the fact that tomorrow was the very last day of *Aurora*. At two o'clock there would be a matinee, and then the final closing performance at eight. Did her parents know this? No. Would they care if they did? No. How she wished she could talk to Philip!

Mrs. Pearl sipped her wonton soup delicately before she spoke. "Emily. Your father and I are so worried."

"They're not going to send Grandma to jail," Emily said. "That would be ridiculous."

"Not 'bout her," Mr. Pearl called. Having his hand in his mouth reduced him to caveman speak. " 'Bout *you*."

"There has been an awful lot of lying going on," Mrs. Pearl said. "We understand that you're sixteen now and entitled to some privacy, but this was too much. And all that money!"

"Unacceptable!" her father said with effort as he headed upstairs. "I take Motrin. Go call dentist."

Mrs. Pearl sighed and turned back to Emily. "We feel you need some help sorting out your values right now, Emily, and your father and I don't know where to begin. This drama club show of yours—it gave us an idea." She paused to pick up her chopsticks, though her food was probably cold by now.

"Tomorrow," Mrs. Pearl said, "we're taking you to see Rabbi Levin."

The bartender looked twice at Philip's fake ID but ultimately poured him a pint of Sam Adams. It didn't take long for the beer to start going to Philip's head, since he hadn't eaten and wasn't accustomed to drinking in the first place. Ian perched on the edge of the piano bench next to the pianist, leafing through a fat binder full of sheet music and chatting flirtatiously about which keys sat well in his voice and his pre-ferred tempo for each song.

The lighting in Don't Tell Mama was pleasantly dim, but if you positioned yourself carefully, you could find a little pin spot of light at each table, just enough to read by. Philip sipped his beer and leafed through the spreadsheets from Miss O'Malley's file. He found comfort in the columns of figures, the beautiful order and predictability of it all. A show was ei-ther in the red or in the black. One thing or another; there was no middle ground. No wondering. No waffling. Philip knew it was a high compliment to say of an actor that one would pay to hear him read the phone book, and now he understood why: numbers had no subtext.

"So hey," Ian said, sliding gracefully into his seat. "I'm still hornswaggled to find you here in town, after dark no less. And don't be offended, but you look a tad like shit. Is everything okay?"

Philip shrugged. "There was some stuff going on at home. I just needed to get out." Suddenly words were coming out of his mouth that he hadn't planned to say. "They keep hammer-ing me about whether or not I'm gay," he said. "And I think Emily's mad at me, too."

Ian's eyes opened wider, but he just nodded. "I hear you. What happened with Em? You guys are so tight."

Philip groaned and put his head in his hands. "I asked her to be my girlfriend. Stupid, stupid, stupid."

"LaGuardia! You're on!" It was the pianist, gesturing to Ian.

"Oh," said Ian. "My. To be continued." He jumped up and smoothed his pants. "What you need is a song. This one's for you."

"What is it?"

Ian's eyes twinkled with mischief. "Something even Philip Nebbling has never heard before."

With that, Ian went to the piano and positioned himself behind the mike stand. "Ladies and gentlemen," he intoned. "Welcome to Don't Tell Mama's piano bar, home of the stars of today, tomorrow, and even yesterday. But she's not working this shift." There was some rude laughter from the audience. "I will now perform, for the first time ever in public: selections from *Inferno! The Musical.*" He held up a hand to stifle the audience's reaction, and spoke with solemn reverence. "Based on the epic poem—by Dante."

There were some appreciative hoots and a bit of clapping. One person said, "He's kidding, right?" loud enough to be overheard, which prompted a fresh wave of laughter. Then the pianist launched into the introductory vamp, and soon the patrons at all the nearby tables were listening in spite of themselves.

The first song was "Beatrice, Beloved, Be Mine," followed by "Virgil Knows the Way" and "It's a Helluva Fix We're In":

> *Hot up top,*
> *Cold below,*
> *Cries of torment wherever we go,*
> *So much suffrin' is really a sin,*
> *It's a helluva fix we're in!*

Ian was a terrific performer. He had a clear, tuneful voice, and he was wonderfully expressive. There was an energetic round of applause when he was done.

"Thank you!" Ian said. "I thank you! Dante thanks you! Thank you all, very much!" Ian grabbed a cocktail napkin and blotted his forehead as he returned to the table. "Oh my God," he said, sliding back into his seat next to Philip. "I think that was the first time you've ever heard me really sing. You better say something nice! I'm feeling all naked now."

Philip stared at Ian as if he were seeing a ghost.

"Who wrote those songs?" he said.

Ian shrugged. "I told you," he said. "Some friend of that crazy director's. Whassup?"

Philip hated to sound arrogant, but he knew what he knew, and he'd known it since the end of the first refrain of "Beatrice, Beloved, Be Mine." "This director—do you know him? Is he your acting teacher?"

"Heaven forbid! No, he's a guy they brought in. Eeeeeevil Smeeeeeeeeeve. They want us to get used to working with pros, so they hire these freelance weirdos all the time."

It couldn't be the beer, could it? Even as he thought this, Philip knew it wasn't. He'd heard this songwriter's work before. Many times before, in fact. Philip knew this the way an art expert could recognize a real Van Gogh from a brushstroke and tell a forgery at a glance. It was there like a fingerprint, in the vamp, the chord progressions, the twisted little rhymes.

" 'Smeeeeeeeeve.' " The name sounded familiar, too. Philip started rummaging through the file that still lay on the table, freshly anointed with a big circular beer stain. "How do you spell that?" he asked.

"With an 'S,' for merde-head. Show-canceler. Supersensitive sourpuss, that's how I'd spell it," Ian said. "Hey, didn't you hear the part about me feeling naked? Are you gonna say something about my performance or not?"

Philip was staring at the papers he'd stolen from Stevenson's office. He scanned quickly.

"With an 'A,' " he said softly. "It's spelled with an 'A.' "

And then—call it an overwhelming moment—Philip leaned across the table and kissed Ian right on the lips.

"You were fantastic," he said. "You're a star."

"Lawd, honey." Ian grinned in delight. "You're full of surprises tonight."

"I gotta go." Philip grabbed his bag.

"You're leaving? Why? Was it my singing?" said Ian, bewildered. "My breath?"

"I have to tell Emily something," said Philip, and he ran out the door.

24

"EMILY'S BAT MITZVAH" (FLASHBACK SEQUENCE)

My Life: The Musical
1992. Music, lyrics, and book
by (and starring) Emily Pearl, as herself

Saturday. Two performances left.

In the middle of the second act of *Aurora*, there was a flashback sequence that never failed to give Emily chills.

Its beginning was signaled by the leaping, twirling entrances of a chorus of dancers, all dressed in variations of Aurora's signature outfit: poncho, fishnet tights, leg warmers, stiletto-heeled boots, bustier, and mittens. Awesome strobe-light effects launched the second act into a toe-tapping journey through the fragmented landscape of Aurora's fictional psyche.

Emily had flashbacks, too. It happened while she was drifting off to sleep, or muddling in vain through her trigonometry homework. And it was happening right now, during Saturday-morning services at the Rockville Centre Reform Jewish

Synagogue. Emily's parents had dropped her off to endure the service alone while they went to pick up Grandma Rose at the hospital, and then to a meeting with their lawyer to discuss the "case": *Rose Pearl and Stan Lefkowitz v. the State of New Jersey, Cossack Division.*

After the service Emily had an appointment to see Rabbi Levin privately for "spiritual guidance," as her mother had described it. Emily hadn't met with the Rabbi alone since they were preparing for her bat mitzvah, three action-packed years before, and her thoughts kept straying back to that time.

If my life were a musical, thought Emily, *this would be the big flashback number, like the one in the second act of* Aurora. Back, back we would go . . . back to the night of Emily Pearl's bat mitzvah . . . the night it all began. . . .

No doubt about it: thirteen-year-old Emily Pearl had made out like a bandit at her bat mitzvah.

She stared at the pile of checks on the dining room table, at the piece of ruled paper in front of her, at the nubby chewed-upon pencil next to the free solar-powered calculator she'd received as a promotional gift with one of her magazine subscriptions.

"How's it going, Em?" Mrs. Pearl was still wearing the diaphanous peach-colored dress she'd purchased just for today. She looked kind of nice, but Emily wished her mother would change so the bat mitzvah day could officially be over. It had definitely been fun, but now she was tired and her head hurt from all the music and attention and too many sweets.

"Oh my!" Mrs. Pearl was looking over Emily's shoulder. "Are you sure? That's an awful lot."

Emily had never been a straight-A math student, but she'd

been extracareful and had used the calculator. "I'm sure, Mom," she said. "I did it twice."

"You forgot this one," Mrs. Pearl murmured, stroking her daughter's hair. "See?"

Mrs. Pearl was right. A small envelope had slipped away from the pile, and was now half hidden under the pretty lace table runner the Pearls used only on holidays and special family occasions, like today.

Emily picked up the envelope and opened it carefully. "It's from Uncle David," she said.

Crazy Uncle David, of the implausible business schemes and erratic fortunes. He'd had a fabulous time at the party, kicking off his shoes and sock surfing with abandon all over the slippery dance floor of the temple's reception hall, much to the delight of Emily's friends.

Emily read the note.

> I'm so proud of you, Emily! Here's a present I think you'll enjoy. My gut tells me it's gonna be a hit.
>
> Love,
> Your Crazy Uncle David

In her hands, courtesy of her crazy uncle, Emily held two tickets to the first preview of a brand-new Broadway show, which started performances the following Tuesday and was scheduled to open at the end of the month. Emily skimmed the Arts and Leisure section of the Sunday *Times* every week, but she had never heard of this show.

It was called *Aurora*.

★　　★　　★

"So this show—*Aurora*—it's very special to you?"

Emily slumped in her chair and stared at the carpet. Rabbi Levin toyed with the end of his ballpoint pen. What a far cry from the joyful meetings they'd had in preparation for her bat mitzvah! All that talk of service to others, the dawn of self-knowledge, a spiritual journey about to begin. Three years later and here she was: selfish, deceitful, and hopelessly unrepentant. She said nothing, and the silence sat heavily between them.

"Emily," Rabbi Levin finally said. "You know what attorney-client privilege is?"

"Yes," she said. Philip had told her about it. It meant that lawyers with guilty clients couldn't rat on them and had to defend them even though they knew what really happened.

"You and I, we have Rabbi-Emily privilege," he said, smiling. "What you say here, stays here. You understand?"

"Didn't my parents tell you what I did?" Emily asked.

Rabbi Levin glanced at an index card on his desk. "You spent, let's see, a little over five thousand dollars on tickets to a show," he said, as if this were perfectly normal. "A Broadway musical?"

"Yes," said Emily. "A musical called *Aurora*."

"I've heard of it," said the Rabbi. "Tell me about it."

So Emily told him, much more than she intended to, in fact. She told him how seeing a performance of *Aurora* filled her with a kind of joy that she could never, ever get enough of—the music, the dancing, the familiar yet always thrilling story of a disadvantaged young woman's journey to stardom, love, heartbreak, and redemption.

She told him how sometimes the waves of love that flowed

between the audience and the actors were so strong, Emily believed they were on the verge of becoming visible.

She told him how seeing *Aurora* always happened in a crowd, but was strangely private as well, as if everyone in the theatre—the actors, the musicians, the stagehands, the ushers, the 1,545 audience members whom the Rialto could seat when the show was sold out—all of them were there just for Emily, to help create the magic feelings that filled her insides the moment the music began to play.

She told him how during and immediately after the show she felt—no, in those *Aurora*fied moments she *knew* down to the bone that she, Emily Pearl, was a unique and spectacular individual, destined for a life of joy and achievement, and yet she was also an inextricable and beloved part of something much, much larger than herself.

It was, without question, the best feeling she'd ever had. But then the feeling would fade, and she needed to see the show again to recapture it. And with the help of some creative financing and a little harmless deception, she had seen it, again and again.

And tonight it would be gone, forever.

She finished talking, and Rabbi Levin sat quietly, nodding. When he spoke, his words were slow and deliberate.

"So, for you," said the Rabbi, "this musical was, in fact, a religious experience. It evoked in you a holy bliss—transcendence, some call it."

"It's a really good show," said Emily.

"Somehow, this musical—*Aurora*, you said the name was?—caused you to see yourself as sacred, irreplaceable, and uniquely loved by God, yet also inextricably bound together with all your brothers and sisters in the human family."

"I guess," Emily said. "It won the Tony."

"It taught you that life is ephemeral—the moments happen and are gone, and we have to cherish each one as it passes." Rabbi Levin's eyes were sparkling. He was on a roll. "It's what we do, who we are *right now* that defines us. Not our memories, not our fantasies—but *this moment*, now."

"Sure," said Emily. Rabbi Levin had lost her. "I get that."

"And lastly," said the Rabbi, his voice starting to resonate the way it did when he was speaking in the temple, "you learned that one taste of spiritual bliss is not enough. You have to keep going back, again and again, to drink from the well of holiness. It's a life's work, Emily. The Hindus say it takes more than one life—one life could never be enough to achieve nirvana, as they call it."

"I thought Nirvana was a band," said Emily.

"It was. And they rocked, let me tell you!" Rabbi Levin looked like he might jump up and start playing air guitar, but then he composed himself. "You know, Emily, everything you learned from *Aurora*—you can get all of that right here, in the synagogue. Every weekend. No ticket required."

"If I come to temple every week, do you think my parents would forgive me for what I did?" Emily asked. "Do you think they'll ever trust me again?"

"Your parents are good people, but forgiveness and trust can be hard," said Rabbi Levin kindly. "That can be their spiritual work, okay? You worry about your own. Emily, Emily, Emily," he said, tapping his head with the pen. "There's a play you would like, I just thought of it. It's called *Our Town*. The girl in it is named Emily, just like you."

Rabbi Levin went on talking about *Our Town*, but Emily was not really paying attention—

". . . *after the character of Emily dies she gets to visit the world of the living once more, and it's terribly sad because she can't change anything* . . ."

Something was going on outside the window to Rabbi Levin's study, but he had his back to it, so only Emily could see, as he droned on about the play—

". . . *and she comes to appreciate that the beauty of life is precisely because of how fleeting it is, how each moment is precious* . . ."

It was Philip outside the window, waving and jumping. His head bobbed up and down over the thick hedge. He was holding—what? A sign, it looked like.

". . . *of course it's all very New England, very Protestant, in fact; in some ways it's the least Jewish play ever written!* . . ."

Emily could almost read the sign, but she didn't want the Rabbi to notice her gawking out the window. She kept taking quick, furtive glances.

I KNOW

it said.

I KNOW WHO

I KNOW WHO WROTE

I KNOW WHO WROTE AURORA

was what the sign said.

"Rabbi Levin!" Emily said, interrupting. "I am so sorry. I have to use your bathroom, may I be excused?"

Philip only had to wait a minute before he saw Emily's head craning out the bathroom window, scanning the yard, looking for him. He scurried behind the bushes, keeping low to the ground, until he reached the shrubs outside the bathroom.

Philip was tall and Emily was not, but now, with her hanging half out the bathroom window and him standing on the dirt, they could see eye to eye.

"Philip! Grandma Rose and Stan got arrested, and Stan had a fake driver's license and it's a big mess!" she whispered, all in a rush. "And my parents found out about us seeing the show, and the money we borrowed, and—"

"I know," he said. "I e-mailed you last night and left messages on your phone and this morning I went by your house and no one was there, so finally I called the hospital. Grandma Rose told me where to find you."

"I tried not to say anything about Mark, but they're going to see the lawyer today and I'm sure it'll all come out. Oh, I don't want you to get in trouble, Philip, I'm so sorry—"

"Emily," he said, practically laughing. "I know who wrote *Aurora*. His name is Smeave. And look."

He was digging around in his pocket as he spoke and produced a slim, rectangular piece of stiff paper, which he handed to Emily.

"Oh! Oh!" said Emily, almost falling off her perch. "That's an *Aurora* ticket!" Her face crumpled. "For last night."

"I know," said Philip. "Read what's on the back."

It was a string of words, written in Philip's own neat handwriting, marching like a column of numbers down the back of the ticket.

SMEAVE
SMAEVE
SAMEVE
SAEMVE
SAEVME
SAVEME

"SAVEME? Dear God!" It wasn't the kind of thing Emily often said, but there had been a lot of talk of religion today. "SAVEMEFROMAURORA *wrote the show?* SAVEME *is* Aurora?"

"Yes."

Emily felt faint. "And he's not Mr. Henderson?" *Not Aurora the show, not Aurora the person.* Mr. Henderson's voice reverberated inside her head. *I don't want you write about the aurora borealis. . . .*

Philip put the ticket back in his pocket and smiled. "No, he's not. Though sometimes he works at a high school."

The most obnoxious automotive honk Emily had ever heard blasted from the street. Philip glanced over his shoulder. "That's our ride. Come on."

"Our ride?" Without protest, Emily let Philip lift her out of the bathroom window and place her on the ground.

"Stan let Mark hold the keys to the Winnebago." Philip shrugged. "Beats walking, right?"

25

"MIRACLE OF MIRACLES"

Fiddler on the Roof
1964. Music by Jerry Bock, lyrics by Sheldon Harnick,
book by Joseph Stein

BwayPhil: Attention, Aurorafans! The countdown to the final performance of Aurora has begun!

AURORAROX: today, at 8 PM
at the Rialto Theatre
we are now at—

BwayPhil: Six.

AURORAROX: thanx BwayPhil!

AURORAROX: six hours and counting!

SAVEMEFROMAURORA: Well, hello there.

AURORAROX: well, howdy, saveme!

SAVEMEFROMAURORA: You two seem rather jolly. I thought you'd
be down in the dumps.

BwayPhil: Why?

SAVEMEFROMAURORA: Because ye olde show of shows is biting the dust.

SAVEMEFROMAURORA: You know: so long, Aurora ol' pal, we hardly knew ye.

BwayPhil: It's just a show, SAVEME.

AURORAROX: exactly.

AURORAROX: but YOU sound a bit glum.

AURORAROX: we would have guessed you'd throw a party

SAVEMEFROMAURORA: Yeah well, it's always sad when something ends.

SAVEMEFROMAURORA: Even something tacky.

BwayPhil: Tacky but profitable, right?

SAVEMEFROMAURORA: Ha! It's no Lion King, believe me—

SAVEMEFROMAURORA: Show struggled to recoup, it's got a big cast, makes it expensive to run.

SAVEMEFROMAURORA: Don't imagine you know what recoup means.

BwayPhil: Sure we do.

AURORAROX: but six percent of the gross

AURORAROX: must have added up

AURORAROX: to something, right?

BwayPhil: What we don't know is whether we should call you Aurora,

BwayPhil: or Mr. Smeave.

AURORAROX: or maybe you'd prefer A.?

BwayPhil: It's a helluva fix you're in, when you think about it . . .

SAVEMEFROMAURORA:

SAVEMEFROMAURORA: speechless

SAVEMEFROMAURORA: how did you . . . ?

BwayPhil: Don't ask too many questions, please.

AURORAROX: hee hee

SAVEMEFROMAURORA: life passing before eyes

SAVEMEFROMAURORA: the internuts will have a field day

SAVEMEFROMAURORA: you have no idea what a catastrophe

SAVEMEFROMAURORA: head hurts, feeling dizzy

SAVEMEFROMAURORA: this is how people have strokes

BwayPhil: RELAX! If you don't want us to tell anyone, we won't.

SAVEMEFROMAURORA: You must want something. What do you want?

BwayPhil: We just want to meet you.

AURORAROX: and find out why you've been so unhappy with the show

BwayPhil: Because we love it.

AURORAROX: and we think you're amazing

BwayPhil: And we've been through a lot for the show.

AURORAROX: A LOT

AURORAROX: and it just would be nice to know

AURORAROX: if it was all worth it.

BwayPhil: That's all.

SAVEMEFROMAURORA: That's all?

AURORAROX: yes

BwayPhil: Yes.

SAVEMEFROMAURORA: Damn.

SAVEMEFROMAURORA: You had to go and say all the right things.

BwayPhil: What do you say, Mr. Smeave?

AURORAROX: please?

AURORAROX: you can trust us

AURORAROX: we didn't tell anybody about your "hunch"

AURORAROX: remember?

SAVEMEFROMAURORA: Unlike some people! I could strangle that Marlena. What I get for being nice.

SAVEMEFROMAURORA: But that's water under the bridge, now.

SAVEMEFROMAURORA: thinking

SAVEMEFROMAURORA: Okay.

SAVEMEFROMAURORA: You know the Toys 'Я' Us? The one in Times Square with the Ferris wheel inside?

BwayPhil: Sure.

SAVEMFROMAURORA: Four o'clock, upstairs by the animatronic dinosaur. If you bring anyone with you the deal's off.

AURORAROX: awesome!!! Thank you!!!!

BwayPhil: How will we know you?

SAVEMEFROMAURORA: Wear mittens. I'll find you.

During the whole careening ride from Philip's house to Emily's, with Mark whooping and hollering at the wheel of the dinged-up but still drivable Winnebago, Emily had Philip recite the Rockville Centre train schedule. Mark had begged to drive them into the city, but the thought of him maneuvering the RV through Times Square was too terrifying to contemplate.

In theory it would work: they would catch the 3:02 into the city, meet SAVEME at four o'clock, then Emily would make the 6:39 from Penn Station back to Rockville Centre and be at school in plenty of time for the show. What an inconvenient night to be making her stage debut! She fully expected that the thrill of meeting Aurora—the *real* Aurora!—would knock every bit of Mr. Henderson's *Fiddler* choreography out of her head, but she didn't care. She could always fake some steps from the movie version; those she knew by heart.

There was a tiny element of risk in stopping at Emily's house on the way to the train station, but the mitten thing seemed important and Philip didn't have any at D-West. Besides, Emily's parents were supposed to be at the lawyer's office with Grandma Rose, so the house would be empty. They'd head in, grab the mittens, and be long gone before any parental interference could occur.

Mom, Dad, I know I'm grounded, but somebody incredibly important is going to meet me and Philip at an animatronic dinosaur in Times Square at four o'clock and can I go and please please have money for the train, please?

No. Grounded or not, it was better to just go and suffer the consequences. She could apologize later, beg forgiveness, be confined to her room for the rest of her life. This was too important.

Just to be sure, Mark let them off a block away and Emily had Philip go around the side of the house and peek in the window of the garage to see if the car was gone. It was. Only then did they approach the front door.

There was a small flower arrangement sitting on the steps, still wrapped in clear plastic and wrapping paper from the florist. Philip bent to pick it up.

"It's probably for Grandma Rose," Emily said. "Better leave it there." She put her key in the lock and cautiously opened the door.

Lights off. Empty rooms. "All clear," she said to Philip. "Keep an eye out while I get the mittens."

Philip took up his post by the door as Emily trotted upstairs. She quickly found what she was looking for in the back of her closet, in a box marked HATS & GLOVES. Mrs. Pearl tended to be very organized about things like that. Emily raced downstairs again.

"Got 'em," she said to Philip. "We'd better get out of here." She was halfway out the door before he could stop her.

"Wait! The flowers are for you," Philip said. "Look."

"For me?" Emily reached for the card stapled to the top of the paper. "To Miss Emily Pearl," the envelope read, in a familiar red script. Emily opened the card.

Emily,

Thank you for being an "A+" trouper! But Lorelei says her ankle is much better and she insists on performing tonight. See you at the show?

Mr. Henderson

She stared at the card in her hand. "What is it?" Philip asked.

"A miracle," Emily said. "Hang on a minute. I just changed my mind about something." She picked up the arrangement and carried it into the house, placing it prominently on the coffee table in the center of the living room. Then she turned back to Philip. "Can I borrow a Sharpie?"

Philip reached into his jacket pocket, pulled out one of his ever-present markers, and handed it to Emily. She turned the card over and wrote on the back.

Dear Mom & Dad,

I'm going into the city with Philip. Something has happened that is the most important thing that's ever happened in my life. Not only that, but it is part of my spiritual journey. If you have any questions please call Rabbi Levin.

No time to explain but I hope you can trust me that it is the right thing to do.

She paused for a moment, then added:

Also, tell Grandma Rose that the cheerleader is a pro after all (see other side of card for details).

Love,
Emily

Emily put the card next to the flowers. "Okay," she said. "Now we can go."

"What's the miracle?" Philip asked, puzzled.

Emily smiled. "I'm getting an A-plus in Mr. Henderson's class."

26

"THERE'S NO BUSINESS LIKE SHOW BUSINESS"

Annie Get Your Gun
1946. Music and lyrics by Irving Berlin, book by Herbert Fields and Dorothy Fields

Saturday. One performance left.

The animatronic T. rex on the third floor of Toys "R" Us was as big as a house, with bloodred eyes that stared right at you as the thing lurched around with lifelike, reptilian movements. To Emily it looked like it was about to burst out of the *Jurassic Park* exhibit, hurl itself down the escalators and through the plate-glass storefront, and go on a rampage through Times Square.

Every few minutes it roared, in deafening, floor-shaking surround sound. One would think the parents and nannies would know not to shove their two-year-olds up close to this thing, but apparently not.

"Rrrrrrrrroooowwwwwwwwwwwwwww!" roared the T. rex.

"Waaaaaaaaaaaaaaaaaahhhhhhh!" screamed the children.

"I don't know which is more frightening," commented a man who stood near Philip and Emily. It was 3:59 and they were waiting, exactly as instructed. "The kids, or the dinosaur."

"They're just scared," said Emily.

"Parents are so clueless sometimes," said Philip.

"True," said the man. He was short and round, in high-water pants, a green sports coat, and glasses. "Look how over-dressed those kids are. I'd be cranky too if I were in a snowsuit. It's so overheated in these stores."

Emily and Philip both nodded as they scanned the crowds, looking for the very special person who was somewhere nearby. Emily tried hard not to envision the rotund little man dressed in a baby's snowsuit, but it was futile.

"You think it's hot?" the man said again.

"Yeah," said Emily. He was kind of a weirdo. Maybe they should go wait in the next aisle. Anyone as fabulous as the real Aurora undoubtedly would be easy to spot, even from ten feet away.

"Then why," the man asked, in a low, "gotcha" tone of voice, "are the two of you wearing *mittens?*"

Ever so slowly, Philip and Emily held up their mittened hands, like it was a stickup. "You must be Phil," said the man. "And his faithful friend Roxy, I presume?"

"Oh my God," said Emily. "Oh my God."

Philip looked down at the man, unavoidably noticing the comb-over swirling around his bald spot. "Are you—Aurora?" Philip stammered.

"My name is Albert." The man's eyes darted around, rat-like. "Albert Smeave."

"Rrrrrrrrrooooowwwwwwwwwwwwww!" bellowed the T. rex.

The only place to sit down in the whole store was on the Ferris wheel, so Albert bought a strip of tickets and the three of them climbed into one of the small, garish cars, each one shamelessly promoting a toy based on a television character or a television character based on a toy.

They boarded in the basement level of the store and soared around and around, swooping upward past the stuffed animals and the Hot Wheels, and lingering at the tippy-top right in front of the glass elevators filled with awestruck shoppers. The glass elevators went up and down, the Ferris wheel went round and round, and Philip felt like he might throw up.

"Thank you for buying the tickets, Mr. Smeave," said Emily. She meant for the Ferris wheel, but Philip thought that this guy Smeave might well say the same to her.

Albert waved away her thanks. "Let's be honest," he said. "I'm a wealthy man. All because of *that show*."

"Tell us," said Emily as the wheel lurched them forward and up. "Tell us who you really are."

Albert shrugged. "I'm just a guy from Illinois," he said. "Aurora, Illinois. That's my hometown. I was your average miserable kid, until I joined the drama club at school. It changed my life."

"The drama club?" asked Emily dubiously. "Really?"

"Sure," said Albert. "Pretending to be other people somehow made me feel like I knew who I was. I was Nicely-Nicely Johnson in *Guys and Dolls*. Herbie in *Gypsy*. Arpad in *She Loves Me*. They were character parts, but I always stopped the show." He smiled at the memory. "Still, it wasn't enough for me, so I started to put on my own shows. Pretty soon I discovered that writing was my passion."

"Our school's doing *Fiddler* this year," said Philip, clutching the safety bar and fighting the urge to retch. "Emily's in it, sort of." The car ahead of them was decked out with characters from *Jimmy Neutron,* and from Philip's perspective the leering, painted face of Jimmy was staring at him from over Albert's shoulder.

"I'm just an understudy," Emily said, suddenly feeling a twinge of disappointment that she wasn't going on.

"*Fiddler!*" Albert cried. "See—if I could have written *that* show! Or any of the great ones! *West Side Story! Oklahoma! Gypsy!*" Albert sounded reverent. "But to make it big with this . . . professional embarrassment . . ."

Emily wanted to leap to *Aurora*'s defense, but an ocean of pent-up, unspoken suffering was ready to burst out of Albert, and he spent the next full revolve of the Ferris wheel in nonstop confessional mode.

All he'd ever wanted was to write serious, literary theatre, he told them. Like *Inferno! The Musical.* Now his dream was to complete an historical epic about the Black Death.

"It's called *Plague!*" Albert sighed. "With an exclamation point. I slave for years on these projects, but no one understands them! No one will put them on! I wheedle little student productions here and there, just so I can hear my work, but— amateurs! It's always a disaster." The Ferris wheel spun them upward and stopped. Albert slumped in despair. "And I wrote *Aurora* over spring break my second year at college, because everybody else had a girlfriend or a boyfriend or a trip to Florida and I was broke and alone. It's sophomoric crap, and look what happened."

They were suspended at the top now, and Philip was paralyzed with the same fear that had gripped him at the top of the Space Needle. He was afraid to look out of the car.

"That's why I can't put my name on it," said Albert. "If people know I wrote *Aurora*, that's all they'll want from me ever again. My chances for a career as a serious dramatist will be ruined."

"But we *like* it, Mr. Smeave," said Emily. "It makes us happy. Doesn't that mean anything?"

"Kids!" Albert said, leaning forward so suddenly he rocked the car they were in. "Artistically, I am a *failure*. I want you to know this. Find another hero, okay?"

"It's too late for that," said Philip suddenly. Emily looked like she was about to cry, and he was feeling as green as the stack of Kermit dolls they kept whooshing past, but this cruel dismissal of the show they loved so dearly had to be refuted. "It's much too late, Mr. Smeave. We've already given everything we have for *Aurora*, and you—you won't even put your name on it."

"What the hell are you talking about?" said Albert.

So Philip and Emily told Albert the whole saga, starting with Emily's bat mitzvah and encompassing all that happened afterward: the joy and lies and borrowed money, the uncounted miles on the Long Island Railroad, Lester and Morris and the Closing Toe, Grandma Rose and Stan's failing eyesight and the Winnebago, Mark and his improbable romance with Stephanie, Ian's performance at Don't Tell Mama, not to mention a nasty bruise on the arm of a New Jersey state trooper.

By the time they were done, Albert Smeave was stunned. He considered himself a skilled storyteller, but only real life could cook up a tale as preposterous as this one. Philip and Emily sat there looking at him with big wet eyes, like two waifs in a black velvet painting.

"Well." He tried acting gruff to cover up how touched he was by their story. "Huh. That's some wacky tale."

"And so you know, we'll come see whatever you write," Philip added, with conviction.

"Yes," said Emily. "We're fans of yours."

"You are?" Albert was confused. "You mean, you'd come see something I wrote even if it wasn't crap—I mean, *Aurora?*"

"Of course," said Emily, as if it should be evident by now. "You're our favorite writer."

Philip wanted to sit up straight and proud, but these cars were designed for little kids and his head would bump against the top if he did that. With as much dignity as he could muster in a hunched-over position, he pulled an *Aurora Playbill* out of his backpack. It was the one from his birthday, with the signature of every single member of the *Aurora* cast on it. He offered it to Albert.

"Please," he said. "Do you need a Sharpie? I have tons."

Albert looked at the *Playbill* as if it were crawling with lice. "Phil. Roxie," he said, his voice cracking. "You guys turned out to be a lot nicer than I expected. But I hope you understand why—I can't, I just can't put my name on that."

"We understand," said Philip. "Just sign it 'Aurora.' That way you can keep your secret."

" 'Aurora'? But that would mean nothing!" said Albert. "Anyone could write that!"

"But you're not anyone! You're the real Aurora," Emily declared. And he was! She could see it now, just by looking in his eyes: the wounded idealism, the capacity for struggle and sacrifice, the creative fire burning inside. It was all there. "It's who you truly are," she said, touching his hand. "Even if no one knows it but us."

Albert looked at them, with their shiny, somewhat zitty adolescent faces beaming at him, all innocence and trust. *Jeez,* he thought. *The boy's got nothing, and the girl spends her grandma's money on my stupid little show. And they don't even look sorry.*

Before he could change his mind, he scribbled something on the *Playbill* and shoved it back at Philip.

"Albert Smeave," Philip read, with wonder. "You signed it Albert Smeave. Are you sure?"

Albert shrugged, but his heart was pounding in his chest. "If *Aurora* could mean that much to a couple of nudniks like you, maybe I have nothing to be ashamed of." He sat on his hands before Emily and Philip could see that they were shaking. "Anyway, the show's closing tonight. If I don't own up to it now, when can I? Wait a minute. Maybe you guys want these, huh?"

He patted all his pockets before finding what he was looking for. A slim, white, rectangular envelope: the kind that held tickets.

"There's two in there. Enjoy," he said. "Stephenson's office keeps sending me house seats but I don't want 'em."

Emily and Philip were practically cross-eyed staring at the envelope that dangled in front of them. Neither one of them reached for it.

"No, Mr. Smeave. You should go," said Emily firmly. "But take Philip."

"Take Emily," Philip said, even more firmly and practically at the same time. "You both deserve to be there tonight."

"How about *you* two go," said Albert, grinning and tucking the tickets into Philip's pocket. "I've seen it plenty, and I know how it ends."

The Ferris wheel had returned them to the ground, and it was time to get out. "Anyway, I'm going to go home and write," Albert said. "It's possible you kooky kids have given me an idea."

A miracle! A miracle! A miracle had happened and they were going to see *Aurora* one more time. Tonight, closing night. It was all Emily had wanted, just like the character Emily in *Our Town* was given one last visit to the land of the living. One more time, but *knowing* it was the last time, so she could breathe in every moment and collapse in an overstimulated heap afterward. Philip would be there with her, and the thought made Emily feel happy inside. Happy in a cozy, best-friends kind of way.

"Philip?" Emily asked as they walked together through Times Square. Her hair was all staticky and glued to her face because she kept touching it with her woolly mittens, and she had to peel the strands away from her mouth to talk. "I was thinking about what you said. About me being your girl-friend."

"Really?" said Philip.

"Yes," she said. "Did you mean it?"

"In a way I did," said Philip. They continued walking, Emily taking two steps for every one of Philip's. It was half a block before he spoke again.

"Except there's one thing," he said, as if he were continuing the previous sentence without a pause. "I think there's a chance, maybe, that I might be gay."

Philip stopped walking so he could turn and see Emily's face. She still had a strand of hair stuck in the corner of her mouth. Without thinking, Philip reached over and brushed the hair away from her lips. "I mean, maybe, you know? But I thought you should know."

"Okay," said Emily. In a way she was surprised by what he'd said, but also, in a way, not. "So, maybe we should just stay friends for now? Would that be good?"

"Yes," said Philip. It felt like a weight had been lifted. "That would be good."

Emily felt relieved as well. "We'll always be bosom buddies, Philip," she said. "Always."

" 'Bosom Buddies.' " A huge smile lit up Philip's face. "*Mame*, 1966. Music and lyrics by Jerry Herman, book by Jerome Lawrence and Robert E. Lee."

It was almost seven-thirty.

27

"NEVER BE ENOUGH"

Aurora
2005. Music, lyrics, and book by Albert Smeave

Never be enough,
My love for you could never be enough,
Ten thousand years could never be enough,
To say what's in my heart . . .

There was a huge, buzzing crowd in front of the Rialto Theatre, but the first person Emily and Philip recognized was
Morris. He was standing directly under the marquee, leaning
on a cane. Ruthie was with him, weeping and dabbing her eyes
with a tissue.

"Ruthie! Morris! What happened to you?" Emily asked,
concerned. Ruthie jerked her thumb backward toward the
theatre and sobbed.

"It's the Closing Toe," Morris said, rapping his cane on the sidewalk. "No worries. It'll be fine in a couple of hours."

"Two hours and twenty-one minutes, to be precise," Philip corrected.

"Not tonight." Morris snorted. "Ever been to a closing performance?"

Emily and Philip shook their heads, which Morris seemed to take as an invitation to launch into one of his lectures.

"When a real turkey closes it's hilarious, frankly. The audience is stacked with hard-core flop collectors. They come just so they can say they saw the stinker before it died. Hey, Ruthie—remember *Moose Murders?*"

Ruthie nodded, still crying.

"Man, that stank! Anyway, a flop closing is fun. The more people talk about it afterwards the worse the show gets. But this show . . ." He shook his head. "People love this show. It's gonna get emotional. Figure a two-minute hand after every song, at least."

"Such a tragic night," sobbed Ruthie. "So sad!"

"You think it's sad for us—what about the actors?" Morris said. "Tomorrow they're unemployed. Back to the auditions, the catering jobs, the temp agencies." Morris sighed contentedly and leaned on his cane. "Remember when *Cats* closed? What a party that was. The fur was flying. I was picking whiskers out of my clothes all night."

"This is different." Ruthie sniffed. "This is too soon! *Aurora's* time hasn't come yet!"

"All shows close sooner or later," Emily said gently. "Come on, Philip. We'd better go take our seats."

"You have tickets?" Morris was shocked. "For tonight?"

"Orchestra, eighth-row center," Philip said. "And it's not even my birthday."

Morris was right about the audience's mood. Emily could feel it in the air as she and Philip entered the theatre. Emotions were raw and explosive, a mix of loss and celebration and protest. Some people were already getting sniffly as they took their seats.

But not Emily and Philip. For them, being here was pure, transcendent bliss. There were lumps in their throats and butterflies in their stomachs, but from the depths of themselves they knew—as clearly and certainly as anything could be known—they were where they were meant to be, at exactly the moment they were meant to be there.

It was seven-fifty-nine.

"Cell phone?" whispered Philip. It was their ritual, and not to be omitted. *This is the last time,* Emily thought, *goodbye,* and she dug through her bag until she found the phone.

The light was blinking.

She had a message. She could turn the phone off and check the message later, but she had a whole minute, plenty of time. Emily pressed the voice mail button and listened.

"Hello, Emily? It's Mom. Daddy and I just wanted to say we got your note. We were pretty upset to find out you'd gone into the city without permission."

"That's putting it mildly," her father's voice interjected.

Emily's eyes filled with tears. Philip mouthed: "Who?" She held up a hand and listened.

"But we called Rabbi Levin as you suggested, and he encouraged us to have an open mind. In fact, he was quite adamant that we go see the drama club show tonight anyway, though it seems you're not going to be in it."

"Stan and I are going, too!" That was Grandma Rose in the background now. Mrs. Pearl's voice became muffled.

"Rose, you know it's just a high school production, right?"

"So?" answered Grandma Rose, distant but audible. "They're doing *Fiddler on the Roof* and I should stay home?"

Her mother's voice came back to the phone.

"Anyway, that's where we'll be. I expect we'll see you later. Emily, I hope whatever it is you're doing in the city has turned out exactly the way you want. We love you!"

Click.

Emily turned to Philip. The houselights were starting to go down.

"*Fiddler on the Roof,*" she said, in awe. "My whole family's going to see *Fiddler on the Roof.*"

"What?"

"Tonight. Right now." Emily's eyes were big as moons.

"They'll love it, Emily." Philip squeezed her hand. "It's a great show."

The first notes of the overture to *Aurora* began to play.

Emily looked around the glorious, gilded house of make-believe called the Rialto Theatre and turned back to Philip with a smile. "Yes," she whispered. "It is."

Then they turned their eyes to the stage, where the lights were just beginning to come up.

MY LIFE: THE MUSICAL

BY MARYROSE WOOD

STARRING

EMILY PEARL In a few years Emily hopes to be attending Yale University or someplace just as good. She will major in English, with a minor in theology. Love and thanks to Mom, Dad, Rabbi Levin, Uncle David, and Grandma Rose, and to her best friend, Philip.

PHILIP NEBBLING ran for treasurer of the Eleanor Roosevelt High School drama club and won. He plans to be a theatrical producer someday, and has recently begun to date.

LAUREY AND STUART PEARL were so touched by the final scene of *Fiddler on the Roof* (in which Tevye's inability to forgive his daughter Chava for marrying a Russian soldier prevents him from bidding her a proper farewell, even though they may never, ever see each other again) that they resolved at once to forgive their daughter Emily for what, after all, were fairly harmless transgressions.

ROSE PEARL LEFKOWITZ thought the Tevye in the drama club production of *Fiddler* was not bad. ("He was no Zero Mostel, but what do you want?" she commented. "He's just a kid!")

STANLEY LEFKOWITZ was quite relieved when the State of New Jersey declined to prosecute that little misunderstanding at the truck stop. He was equally relieved that he and his new bride, Rose, honeymooned at a nice hotel in Florida and not in a Winnebago.

DAVID PEARL now runs Uncle David's Broadway Treasures, an eBay-based marketer of theatrical memorabilia. A judicious culling of Emily's and Philip's vast signed Playbill collections easily repaid all monies owed to Mark, but the one-of-a-kind "Albert Smeave" program was deemed much too special to sell.

ALBERT SMEAVE was awarded the Pulitzer Prize for Drama for his epic nine-hour musical, *Fiddling While It Burns*, depicting the fall of Rome. Weak ticket sales were further marred when disgruntled customers believed they had purchased seats for a sequel to *Fiddler on the Roof*. He sold the film rights to *Aurora* for a ridiculously large amount of money.

MARLENA ORTIZ was unavailable to reprise her star turn in the title role in the film of *Aurora* due to schedule conflicts. She is currently launching a European tour to promote the release of her first solo album, called *Marlena, Herself*. Her role in the film will be played by a former *Aurora* chorus dancer named Stephanie Dawson.

CHARLES HENDERSON received an Eleanor Roosevelt High School Teacher of the Year award for his ongoing dedication to the drama club. He has not yet decided whether *Aurora* would be a suitable choice for next year's spring musical, but it's certainly possible.

MARK NEBBLING After being dumped by Stephanie Dawson (her budding film career required her to take a "more strategic approach" to relationships, she explained), Mark had what he describes as a "personal awakening." To his mother's amazement, he gave Mrs. Nebbling enough money to pay off the last of her student loans, got a haircut and a part-time job, and is now attending community college—including the occasional acting class—on a much more regular basis.

LORELEI CONNELLY With her ankle in a cast, Lorelei Connelly bravely performed the role of Hodel in the Eleanor Roosevelt High School drama club production of *Fiddler on the Roof*. Not surprisingly, she brought down the house.

STEVIE STEPHENSON Lackluster ticket sales scotched plans for the Lanerick Rep. With the two stars under contract, however, Stephenson quickly regrouped by mounting a pair of out-of-town revivals: Matthew Broderick will tour midsized American cities in *How to Succeed in Business Without Really Trying*, while Nathan Lane will assay the role of Tevye in a Las Vegas production of *Fiddler on the Roof*. Despite its stature as a classic of stage and screen, *Fiddler* has been trimmed and revised for the Vegas production. "Ninety minutes, no intermission, and no Cossacks!" notes Stephenson. "Why? Because the public *always* prefers a happy ending!"

AUTHOR'S NOTE

Writing *My Life: The Musical* has been incredibly special for me, because the world of Broadway musicals was so much a part of my own teen years and remains very near to my heart.

You see, I was cast in my first Broadway musical when I was eighteen years old. As it turned out, it was my last Broadway musical, too. But what a show to be part of! It was called *Merrily We Roll Along* (1981, music and lyrics by Stephen Sondheim, book by George Furth), and it was directed by one of Broadway's most legendary and innovative directors, Harold Prince.

Quite an auspicious beginning for a drama club geek from the suburbs! I mean, what were the odds? How could a second-year acting student at NYU, with no agent or connections or professional experience, become part of such an illustrious project?

Here's how: I showed up at an open call with a resume I typed the night before (yes, on an actual clackety-clack typewriter) and a photo of myself I paid a dollar for in the passport photo booth in Penn Station. I waited all day with the hundreds of other starry-eyed wannabes who'd shown up.

At the end of the day, no closer to auditioning than when I'd arrived, I tossed my resume and photo into a big black plastic trash bag that the stage manager used to collect head shots from all the kids who hadn't been seen. Tired and defeated, we went home.

Some weeks later, my then-boyfriend, Tom, received a letter in the mail. It was from the *Merrily* casting office. His photo had been plucked out of the trash bag, and would he please come in for an audition on the following Thursday?

What? Him and not me? *They must need boys,* I told myself. I wished him luck that Thursday morning, and off I went to tap class. I was a very poor tapper, mind you, but I liked tap class because I could kid myself that tap wasn't actually dance, but math, since it involved a lot of counting. Dancing I wasn't so hot at, but math I could do.

An hour later I emerged from class, sweaty and gross. The receptionist of the dance studio called me over to his desk and handed me a slip of paper with a phone message on it. The message was from my boyfriend, and I will never forget what it said.

"They want you at the Sondheim audition. Get here before six. Love, Tom."

What could this mean? Was I going to waste time wondering? No! I raced home to my skanky studio apartment in the East Village, where the halls ran thick with roaches and the mailbox was perpetually broken. I showered, dressed, grabbed some sheet music (I only knew one song; it was "I Wish I Were in Love Again" by Rodgers and Hart), and hauled my tapping toes back uptown to a rehearsal studio in the theatre district.

I made it, I think, by five. It still seemed likely that the phone message was some kind of sick joke, but nevertheless I walked up to the person who looked like she was in charge and introduced myself. She laughed heartily—merrily, one might even say. "Maryrose Wood! We've been looking for you!"

(Later it was revealed that I too had been sent a letter offering an audition, a letter that had never been delivered due to my perpetually broken East Village mailbox. A phone message had been left as well, on my answering service, but I never got it because, impoverished acting student that I was, I was behind in my monthly fees and the service was holding all my messages.)

So, to fast-forward a bit—many callbacks later, after I'd sung "I Wish I Were in Love Again" fast, slow, funny, sad, sexy, goofy and every other way they could think of to ask me to sing it, I was one of about two dozen young actors, many of us still teenagers, who got cast in this can't-lose, surefire Broadway hit.

So long, NYU! I was on Broadway now. Could stardom be far behind?

Oh, yes. So very far. Sadly (at the time of its original Broadway production, at least), *Merrily* was a flop. I mean, *flop!* The audience was bewildered, and a steady stream of people walked out during the second act.

The show received some brutal reviews. *New York Times* theatre critic Frank Rich wrote that it was a "shambles," and with the exception of some of the leads, "the rest of the cast is dead wood." Friends joked that I should be glad, because at least he mentioned me by name.

Merrily closed after only sixteen performances. At the last show we sobbed ourselves hoarse during the final number and then showed up at RCA the next morning to record the cast album. (It remains a terrific recording of a marvelous score that has earned a well-deserved "cult" status, and I bet those of you who are ardent musical theatre fans know it well.)

Merrily We Roll Along was a show about how idealistic young people are sometimes forced, and sometimes choose, to abandon their dreams and ideals over time. Some dreams, however, don't die. Twenty-one years after *Merrily*'s Broadway debut, the entire original cast reunited for one night only on the stage of LaGuardia High School. Thrillingly, Stephen Sondheim and Harold Prince were there as well.

After only a few days' rehearsal under the direction of Kathleen Marshall, we performed a concert version of the show to a sold-out audience who went absolutely bonkers with joy. Twenty-one years of history rewrote itself in a night. They loved us, we loved them, and we all loved each other. We were, finally, a hit.

Writing a book is a lot like acting: you get to play all the parts and experience everything your characters feel. For me, working on *My Life: The Musical* and reliving Emily and Philip's over-the-top idealism and their fierce, unconditional love for the theatre was like being given the gift of time travel—the chance to go back, just like the character of Emily in *Our Town*, and look one more time on the sweet innocence of the past, when shows ran forever, everything was bound to be a hit, and stardom was just around the corner.

Life isn't always exactly like a musical, but so what? Idealism is a candle we shouldn't ever let go out. I know Emily and Philip wouldn't, and I hope you never do, either.

May all your dreams come true to *thunderous applause*—

Maryrose Wood

ABOUT THE AUTHOR

While still a teenager, Maryrose Wood made her Broadway debut in the chorus of *Merrily We Roll Along* (1981, music and
lyrics by Stephen Sondheim, book by George Furth). She
went on to act, dance, sing, direct, improvise, and write her
way through many plays and musicals. Her work as a lyricist
and book writer has made her a three-time winner of the pres-
tigious Richard Rodgers Award for new musicals, which is ad-
ministered by the American Academy of Arts and Letters.

Maryrose wrote *Sex Kittens and Horn Dawgs Fall in Love* and
Why I Let My Hair Grow Out. She lives in New York with her
two children and a rather theatrical little dog. And she still
sings—in the shower. Visit her at www.maryrosewood.com.

DATE DUE